Meeting in Madrid

Dorothy Fletcher

CRIMSON
ROMANCE

F+W Media, Inc.

This edition published by
Crimson Romance
an imprint of F+W Media, Inc.
10151 Carver Road, Suite 200
Blue Ash, Ohio 45242
www.crimsonromance.com

CHAPTER 1

The girl in the ITA uniform walked briskly through the main waiting room at Kennedy Field, stopped at a newsstand to buy an evening paper, paid for it, closed up her purse again, then ran lightly down the stairs and opened a door that read Flight Operations. The briefing room was on a lower level and she was, out of training and habit, on time. It was a minute or two before six-thirty when she entered the busy room: report time was an hour and a half before take-off.

Her name was Kelly Jones. She had been flying for ITA for four years and had recently graduated to the status of chief stewardess, or purser. The flight was a 707. She would return on one of the 747's. But on this trip she was top dog and when she entered the room she moved up to the front, making a last adjustment to her cap and tucking her flight bag under her arm.

There were four other stewardesses present; the fifth walked in quickly at exactly half past six. The briefing began promptly and was the usual thing. There were no new campaigns, happily, such as "No white lipstick on this flight." Yes, of course, it could be as petty as that, Even after all these years you had the feeling that you were sized up like a hunk of meat, like a bunny in a Playboy Club. There was still that sense of losing your own individuality. You belonged to the airline and to the hundred odd passengers you were about to service.

But to be fair, you were paid more, per flight time, than you could earn in almost any other field of endeavor. So you stood and suffered the inspection and pretended not to mind.

"Check your coffee makers," Mrs. Tree (who was the briefing instructor) advised. "We're trying a new kind."

A little later she said, "You have two infants."

Groans were stifled.

The only saving grace about night flights (what with all the other draggy circumstances they entailed) was that babes in arms were generally absent. Sensible adults transported babies in the daytime. Two infants meant tears and wails and a good deal of extra service. And as if that weren't enough, Mrs. Tree added, "You have an unaccompanied minor."

Well, Kelly thought. It was going to be a rough flight.

"A child of ten. Male."

Um. Old enough to go to the john himself, Kelly thought. At least there was that.

"Relatives will meet him in Madrid."

Relatives would meet him in Madrid. Meanwhile, it's I who will have to wipe his nose, Kelly reflected, without a change in expression. We will deal with these problems in due time, she told herself; you took it step by step.

"No exceptional passengers otherwise," Mrs. Tree said, in her dry voice. Which meant no movie stars. I didn't expect any, Kelly thought, bored. Night flights were for people who were loath to lose time on travel. The poor bastards counted every penny and started out, practically sleepless, sightseeing on the double.

"Have a good trip," Mrs. Tree concluded and then the Captain, who had spent the last half hour studying the flight plan in the Dispatch Room, walked in for his innings.

It was Norm Robertson, one of the old-timers; Kelly knew him well. A nice guy, one you could depend on. He saw her smile and grinned back.

He greeted them nicely; his voice had warm southern overtones. He was tall, nearly six feet; he had a broad eye-span and sun-tanned skin. He had intelligent, land eyes. He also had six children and he didn't sleep around.

Most of the Captains got Kelly aside and told her in detail how they wanted their roast beef done before they got down to cases.

Captain Robertson, however, was one of the seasoned ones, no nonsense and no gall. He quietly put the girls through their paces: "Tell me how to open the door and put the slide down…"

Some of the new ones, after establishing that they wanted their ribs bloody rare and a double portion of the *mousse au chocolat*, got carried away with it, shooting rapid-fire questions at the girls, coldeyed and mean. But Norman Robertson, who had been doing this for years and years, knew enough to leave it to the cabin crew. He was experienced enough to be sure that the stewardesses were as cautious as he was, that they watched for a grease-fire in the galley or a cigarette thrown by a careless passenger in the waste disposal. The main concern was fire and an airline hostess was as keenly aware of the danger as the cockpit crew.

The routine questions were answered to the point and to the Captain's satisfaction. I wonder, Kelly thought, if passengers had any idea that occasional stewardesses were found wanting and dismissed and a new crew called in. It had happened…and in her time.

The Captain was giving the flight plan now. When that was done he asked who the purser was. Kelly stepped forward.

"Hi," he said. "Seems like I've seen you before."

"Seems as if."

He took her aside and laid down the rules. It was okay; this was one of the old pros. The new crop, the brash, temperamental ones, got in her hair with their insolent assumption of superiority. They could be infuriating with their barked commands: "I don't want you sitting in the lounge. You know the rules, girls."

Sure they knew the rules. A lot of them had more flight time than the captains.

"Looks like it will be choppy about an hour out," Captain Robertson said. "Keep that in mind, honey. You're a pretty girl… Everyone tells you that, right?"

"Always grateful for a kind word. I hear you have a newcomer to the family."

"Three months old now," he said, and got out some color snaps of the newest Robertson. "Smart as a button. Am I boring you, honey?"

"No. Good luck to all of you," she said, sincerely.

But time was passing. "Got your girls assigned to the slides?" he asked, looking at his watch. "If so, I guess we're all set." He turned and saluted, with a pleasant grin, the rest of the girls. "Let's have a good trip," he drawled, and left the room.

"I'm Kelly Jones and I know two of you. Hi, Lucille. Hello, Mimi. Will the rest of you please introduce yourselves?"

"Margot Miller."

"Doris Michaels."

"Wendy Warren."

"All right, let's get with it," Kelly said, and added the inevitable, "Let's have a good trip."

She was the head stewardess, responsible for the cabin crew. It had its onus, no doubt about it, but it paid well, about double that of an ordinary stewardess, which was very good money indeed. You could sock plenty away.

Not like a model, admittedly, but the next best thing to it.

The spring evening was balmy, not really very warm yet; it was only the middle of May. The sky was that lovely color that looked pink one second and violet the next. You didn't want to leave all that dusky beauty and get inside the plane to spend the long, busy night catering to the public. But it was a job, your job, and you did it, if not automatically, at least capably. You put in your time and occasionally you foxed the Establishment.

Air Time averaged around thirteen or fourteen days a month; if you worked it right you managed, at precious intervals, to pull a fiddle, which was, in effect, to outsmart the management. You figured it out painstakingly, studying your monthly patterns, so that every once in a while you had almost half a month layoff time all in one stretch. It wasn't easy and it wasn't cottoned to by the lines, but you could swing it two or three times a year if you were a smart cookie. Kelly was up, on the terminaion of this New York-Madrid flight, for twelve days time off.

A few days in Madrid, and then a short hop to Malaga, after which she would hire a car and tour Andalusia, from Torremolinos to Sevilla. Then she would take an Interline flight to Lisbon and resume duties on the Monster, a 747 headed back to the States.

She would be technically on call, but she could beat that too. Four years' service and expertise helped a hell of a lot. She checked off the new coffee makers with a light heart and heard the welcoming stewardess give her first greeting.

"*Good* evening. May I have your seat number, please?"

• • •

Passengers were labeled, unbeknownst to themselves, "the geese" (or in the case of certain smart alecs of masculine gender, "the goosers"). There were a few standard specimens on tonight's trip. Kelly knew at once, for example, that the party of six in economy (three and three with the aisle between them) were this flight's lushes. Fairfield County…one of them had a copy of the latest novel about hi-jinks in suburbia on his lap. They liked to read about wife-swapping. Maybe they did it and maybe they only dreamed about it, but certainly they enjoyed flipping through the pages to find the really dirty parts.

That little coterie would be hard to take; at least one of them would vomit up the contents of his stomach around three in the morning. "Oy veh, my head," Mr. (or Mrs.) Westport would moan while soliciting her sympathy in the galley. "God. Have you got an icebag or something?"

Then there were the two pinchers. One was traveling alone. A bull-necked beast with white socks and a cheap attache case. "I always did say the ITA girl was the hostess with the mostes'," he'd said to Wendy Warren, with a furtive feel of her backside. "Watch him, he's death," Wendy warned the others. "He'd screw his own mother."

The other satyr was accompanied by his wan, tired wife. A salesman: you could smell it. A small-timer, probably sent economy and paying the difference for first class, out of his own pocket. A real sport. "Listen, let's meet later," he told Kelly. "I can get away, don't worry about that. Where are you staying?"

"I have a date."

"Tomorrow night, then."

"It's just a short layover. Thanks all the same."

They were only half an hour out when a woman passenger began nagging about when was dinner. "Kell, I just can't cope," Mimi Draycott complained. "Every time I pass her she nearly tears my arm off asking me again."

There was also the unaccompanied minor, Richard Comstock, who refused to stay put. He kept wandering back to the galley, brandishing a swizzle stick he'd picked up from the liquor cart. "You're kind of cute, but get the hell back where you belong," Wendy said, pushing him aside.

"Cute? I detest that word," he said, making a face.

"T.S. I'd like to meet you in about ten years."

"You'll be old then."

"You little fink! Get back to your cabin, *baby.*"

He kept trudging back, though, hanging around Kelly, who he figured from the very first was the boss. He spotted her purser's badge. Kelly pigeonholed him without effort: ten years old but the product of a sophisticated environment, top drawer, would prep at Hotchkiss, would go to Haverford or Middlebury or Princeton or Williams, would spend a year or two in Paris, would marry a distant cousin of Jackie Jennedy's, would clip coupons until his death at eighty-five.

Oh, listen, I've seen this kind so often, she said to herself, and to him, "Honey, in about an hour," when he asked, "When do we eat?"

He ran a hand through thick, sunburned blond hair.

His eyes were an ineffable blue. "I'm starved, doesn't that matter?"

"It won't be long."

"Gee."

He jingled some change in his pocket. "Do you have your hair frosted?"

"No, it's naturally this way," she said, giving him a push. Not that she was a crab, far from it, but from takeoff time until landing, there would be no more than a scant hours' rest for her. It was no sinecure. It was a damned hard job.

"Mummy has hers frosted," he volunteered. "You sit there and they put Reynolds wrap around it. It drips. Mummy says it's unbelievably tiresome but it looks nice when it's finished. It takes hours and hours."

"I can think of nothing more fascinating than your mother's hair job, Richard."

"Very funny," he said.

And still he didn't go away. She drew a deep breath and smiled. "How old are you, dear?"

"Ten. Don't pretend you don't know that. I'm a special passenger. They told you how old I was, didn't they?"

"All right, so they did."

"Then why did you ask?" He eyed her. "You're the chief stewardess. Do you make much money?"

"Quite a bit. Will you marry me for my money?"

"I'm betrothed to my cousin Gisela. That was done when we were born. She's Roman. I'm half Italian too. My mother is from an ancient family. It's an excellent lineage."

"Really?"

"We're in the Almanac de Gotha, of course."

"Congratulations."

"Is that an unkind remark?" His eyes narrowed.

"No. Why should you think it was?"

"Because people are envious of others' patrimony," he stated. "I know that for a fact."

Well, Stephen Snob, Kelly thought, but then he turned on the charm again. "You're really awfully pretty," he said. "You have lovely eyes and nice high cheekbones."

"That makes my day," she said, rumpling his hair. "You run along now, sweetie. I have some cooking to do."

"You mean you actually cook? On a stove? I thought—"

"See you later," she said, and turned her back on him. I've put in too much time all in a bunch, she told herself. She was running on her reserves now. The night stretched ahead, endless, it seemed. She would have to watch herself, not to snap at the girls, who—even the ones she knew—tended to resist the authority of the one in charge.

But you must remember, she reminded herself, that when this flight is over, you have twelve whole days vacation. Almost two weeks before going on the job again.

It was a sustaining thought.

• • •

It was in that brief lull after the hot meal was over and the galley cleaned up that Kelly had a chance to palaver with the pet passenger on the flight. The girls had been falling all over him, sneaking him doubles in drinks and wondering if he was a gun-runner. He was in first class and he did look secretive and poker-faced. A little bit like the late Mike Todd, one of Elizabeth Taylor's erstwhile husbands. He had that kind of slightly tough good looks;

the resemblance, though, was mostly in the smoky black hair, eyes and eyebrows. Kelly saw at once why the others found him attractive. He had a kind of leashed animal magnetism.

She ran into him while he was sitting in the lounge, smoking a long and expensive-smelling cigar, and he told her she looked a little beat. She sat down with him, something she rarely did. During the long hours of a flight—particularly a night flight—odd and sundry passengers did their best to claim your exclusive attention, at which times they confided things they wouldn't have dreamed of telling their best friend. This man was intriguing, however, and had made no attempt to soft-talk any of the stewardesses into a date. Not that they had given up hoping.

"Well, I'm a little tired," she admitted.

"Been doing this long?"

"Four years."

"At your age, four years probably seems like a long time."

She put him down as thirty-five, more or less. "I'm not that young," she said.

He didn't say, "You look like a kid, I bet you're not more than twenty," which was the standard gambit with men on the make. She was almost twenty-seven and some days she looked it. Most of the time not, but there were always those discouraging times when you hadn't had enough sleep and then you remembered you weren't as young as you used to be and you still hadn't found what you were looking for.

As a matter of fact he didn't say anything more for a while. He set his half-smoked cigar in an ashtray and the smoke drifted lazily upwards. He stretched and crossed his legs. He was a little on the stocky side, and when he had boarded she had seen that he was only an inch or two taller than herself. She was five foot eight. Just as long as he's not shorter, she reflected, surprising herself.

Would she like to go out with him, then? But he was faintly elusive. He looked different, somehow. The girls were right. There was something about him that set him apart from the ordinary businessman. He looked like a loner; if not a gun-runner, as the girls had been wildly conjecturing, a speculator of some kind. Like a man who took chances. He had that strong, rather hard face. But he also had a sensitive mouth. She found herself looking at his mouth.

There had been a rather long silence, but oddly enough a companionable silence. It was restful to sit here with this quiet man and for the first time in her life she found the smell of a cigar agreeable. He picked it up again, drew on it and then, as the smoke wove around her head, he put it back in the ashtray again. He sighed and leaned back.

"It'll be a long night," he said.

"Can't you sleep?"

"You know how it is. You wait until everyone puts the overhead light out and you start to doze off. Then some insomniac gets tired of tossing and turning so he puts his light on again. Then someone else does. And there are these little pinpoints of light all over. So you decide not to even think about sleep and you make it up when you get to your destination."

He went back to his cigar. "I see our high-toned young passenger has found friends," he remarked, glancing down the aisle.

Kelly followed his look. Young Richard Comstock had indeed found friends; he had been adopted not long out of Kennedy by a middle-aged Spanish couple. Senor and Senora Nascimento, occupying seats in the second row, had taken him under their wing; obviously the boy had also taken a fancy to them. Particularly to the Senora, and at the moment he was sitting patiently with his arms extended as she wound some soft rose-colored wool around his wrists.

"I couldn't be more pleased," she said. "A boy that age all alone can be a first-class headache." She was watching the trio up front. The man was reading something and the woman was winding the wool. Occasionally she would interrupt herself to adjust the long, double string of pearls she wore round her neck. They were the only bright spot in her outfit of austere black. They were good pearls, the best. If it hadn't been for the pearls, and the fact that the Nascimentos were traveling first class, it would have been easy to mistake them for indigent, faded aristocrats without a penny.

They were fine-looking people; both had gaunt, attenuated faces, like El Grecos. They seemed the very essence of old Spain, with their proud noses and hooded eyes.

"I'm Steve Connaught," Kelly's companion said to her. "I should have said that before."

"I'm Kelly Jones."

He held out a hand. The skin of it was dark, almost swarthy, like the skin of his face. There were short black hairs at the wrist. Taking it, a kind of electric shock ran through her, and she knew instantly that if this man were to ask her out she'd say yes. Without thinking further about it. It was something she didn't do all that often, but this time she would.

He didn't ask her, though. They chatted for a while longer and then, because she so wished he'd tap her for a date, her pride got her up off the bench. She was afraid he'd see it in her eyes. She walked down the aisle and talked to the Nascimentos.

"Everything all right?"

"Pair...fect," the Senora said, looking up with a pleased smile. "Thees pretty boy helps me, see that, Senorita? So quiet, such a nice boy."

"You're being very good to him."

"Is a pleasure."

"*Je suis tres bien eleve*," Richard retorted, obviously stung at the inference that he was on sufferance with the Spanish couple.

"See, he speaks French pair...fectly," Senor Nascimento looked up from his book and beamed. He had the wispy, croupy voice of someone much older. Asthma, perhaps. "He speaks a little Spanish, too. A very good pupil."

"They're trying to teach me," Richard explained. "It's a *little* bit like French." He cleared his throat. *"El abogada les explica las difficultados…"*

The Senor and his wife laughed heartily. *"Ah, querido,"* the woman said, fondly.

"Thank you very much for being so kind," Kelly said, and made her way back. There was an occasional request on the way. "You have Fresca, I hope?" a woman asked, and then one or two passengers asked for coffee. Steve Connaught was still sitting cross-legged in the lounge, though he'd finished with his cigar. "Do you want anything?" she asked him.

He leaned his head back. "No. Thanks. Not a thing."

"Well, all right. But if there's…just ask, if you feel like coffee, or Sanka…"

"You're sweet. Thanks, but I don't need a thing."

Kelly had the feeling that his eyes followed her as she went into economy cabin; at any rate her back seemed to tingle, right between the shoulder blades, as she pulled the louver and went through. You're too tired for a date anyway, she told herself, and decided that if Steve Connaught asked any of the girls for a date it would be Wendy Warren. All the girls were nice-looking, but Wendy was the beauty.

So what do I care? she thought.

The Westport tipplers were well on their way to besottedness, the movie was almost over, a few passengers had pillows tucked behind their heads and their overhead lights off, the other stewardesses had just about finished their dinners. The line to the lavatories made working in the galley difficult. When it had thinned out a bit and the head sets were collected and accounted for; when the Little Blue Ball was nearly dark as passengers huddled with coats thrown over them, then there was an opportunity for Kelly to think about her own meal. She ate it rapidly. It tasted like straw and lodged firmly in the center of her gut.

"I want two of you to get some sleep," she said, and assigned Doris and Margot to stay with it while two others slid unobtrusively into back seats. Wendy was assigned up front in first class cabin.

You're a masochist, she told herself. Throwing that beautiful girl at that attractive man's head. You didn't have to do that, did you? So all right, they'll see Madrid together. Due to you, you damned idiot. But if that was all a man wanted…a face and body…

Abruptly, she opened a lavatory door and went in. She washed her hands briskly and then turned to face herself in the mirror. The light was pinkish, designed to be flattering to women, and it was. She looked at herself for a long time. Why did she put herself down? The face that looked back at her was heart-shaped and, as Richard had said, was high in the cheekbones. Her eye span was wide. Her hair was cut short, perhaps too short, and it had cost her plenty at Vidal Sassoon's. There was nothing wrong with her looks.

It was just that every girl wanted to look like Jean Shrimpton, or Wendy Warren. To be ravishing, to make every other girl look sick. And yet, regarding herself gravely, she had a surge of confidence. You sensed things, and Steve Connaught, who had been assiduously wooed by every stewardess in the plane, had sat quietly and companionably with her, only *her*…and she had felt his admiration.

Okay, she thought, and went outside again.

Her trained eyes canvassed the cabin. Everything was quiet, but she knew the babies would start whimpering soon. They were four hours out, with three to go.

She got out her log book, and the night wore on.

She managed to get in almost forty-five minutes rest. Dozing but not able to blank out, she planned ahead. The cockpit crew on this trip was considerate, but that was due to the Captain,

Norman. I hope there isn't a sizeable shortage in my liquor count, she thought restlessly, and again was grateful for the flight crew up front. Some of the newer men, the brash kids who were making it difficult for all of them, frankly confiscated bottles when she wasn't looking. Passengers did their share of stealing too, mostly the small liqueur bottles. They wanted them for souvenirs. There was always someone who cleaned out the soap in the lavatories.

She fingered her small purser's badge, fought to empty her mind, and closed her eyes. A man's face floated in the darkness behind her shut lids. His name was Steve Connaught…with a V or a PH? she wondered, and didn't mind not really sleeping. He had a nice face to think of…and his voice was deep and sexy and rumbling…

Sometimes you had a passenger you wouldn't mind seeing again. It was the ones you didn't want to see again that asked you.

CHAPTER 2

She did sleep after all. Maybe it was only five minutes, but she came out of a dream with a jolt. It hadn't really been a dream, just an atmosphere, a very lovely ambience with the smell of flowers and the touch of a man's hand on her face, stroking, stroking…

"Umm," she mumbled, opening her eyes.

"Do you go to sleep too?"

It was the unaccompanied minor, Richard Comstock, tickling her face with a bit of cotton. In the orange flush of dawn high above the clouds his face looked serene and rested.

"Richard!" She glared at him resentfully.

"I thought you were supposed to guard the plane."

"Go to hell," she almost said, and looked at her watch. It was time to get going anyhow. "I don't suppose it's ever crossed your mind that we girls are human," she snapped at him. "What are you doing back here, you little monster?"

"I'm hungry."

"Ask one of the other girls."

"You're the top man," he said. "I always deal only with the top man."

"Ta da."

He wheedled. "Gee, honest, I need my breakfast. Come on, okay? Give me something to eat."

"Who do you think you are, the Duke of Windsor?"

"When is *breakfast*, that's all I'm asking."

"In half an hour. Does that answer your question?"

"You mean I hafta wait all that time?"

"So does everyone else."

"You're a big help," he said.

"And you're breaking my heart into little pieces. Go back to your Spanish friends."

"They're asleep. Snoring. She snores louder than he does."

"I'm bleeding."

He gave up at last and wandered back to his own territory, while Kelly got up stiffly. In no time at all she was swamped. Sure enough, someone had been sick in one of the johns, hadn't done too good a job cleaning it up and she assigned one of the girls she'd known before, Lucille Kruz, to that unenviable task. It was something that simply couldn't wait for the cleaning crew at the Madrid airport.

"Slobs," Lucille muttered, gritting her teeth. "God damned tourists…"

There was a minor disaster in first class cabin. Richard had somehow gotten caught in Senora Nascimento's beads; they broke and scattered far and wide. There was a great to-do with all present scrambling to retrieve the glossy globules. "It was only an accident," the Senora said, scrambling along with the others. The Senor, in his croupy voice, counted the pearls as they were gathered together. *"Uno, dos, tres…"*

"Nothing to worry," he said triumphantly at long last. "All here, very good, very good."

"Just cheap things," the Senora assured her seat companions. "Silly cheap beads from America."

"To tell you the truth," Richard said to Kelly, "I can't imagine how it happened. I think she broke them herself, the way she she was always yanking at them." He shrugged. "Naturally I'm very sorry." He looked a little worried. "You don't think she's clunked about it, do you?"

"Clunked? What do you read, *The Village Voice?*"

"Because," he said, "I like them very much. Especially her."

"There, she's looking for you," Kelly told him. "I guess she's not clunked."

"That helps," he said. "It was a stupid thing to happen. I'm usually so well-behaved."

He rejoined his friends. "Clumsy me," Kelly heard him saying, and the Senora embraced him and kissed his cheek. She had put the pearls into one of her husband's large linen handkerchiefs, secured the bound kerchief in a hank of her rose-colored wool and dropped the whole into her petit point knitting bag.

A short time before landing, Richard trudged back and announced that Senor and Senora Nascimento would not leave the airport until he was called for. "That's fine," Kelly said, making a mental note to confirm this with the Nascimentos. Otherwise she would feel bound, noblesse oblige, to see to it herself. A child traveling alone…

"Si," the Senor and Senora assured her when she got round to discussing it. "Don't worry about Ricardo."

"You must tell us again your name," the Senor said. "Mama, write it down."

Mama fished and found a silver pen. She fished again and found some paper. "So."

"It's Jones. Kelly Jones. K-e-l-l-y."

"What is this name?" the Senor asked, intrigued. "Kelly?"

"Whimsy on the part of my parents," Kelly said. "I'm not even Irish. Kelly Jones, that's right."

"It was a great pleasure. A charming girl, yes, Mama?"

"*Elegante. Dolce.*"

"Good-bye, Richard."

"Good-bye. I hope you have a great time."

"And you too."

When they put down and the plane emptied out Kelly saw them walking across the field, the three of them together, with Richard's airline bag slung over his shoulder and the Senora's knitting bag clutched in one hand. Not far behind them was Steve Connaught, striding along and looking exciting, the kind of man you'd be a little nervous introducing to your friends but wouldn't care much, deep down, if they approved of him or not. A man who, just walking across the strip with those easy strides, looked different, unusual…and just a little bit dangerous.

The kind of man who, obviously, kept pretty much to himself. Oh well, I wouldn't have gone out with him anyway, she told herself, and tried to convince herself that she meant it.

The per diem was 700 pesetas. Kelly was handed her information papers and the girls received the usual instructions. "Don't drink the water in Spain."

She was relaxed now, deliriously sleepy. "Oh, till about one, I guess," she told Lucille Kruz, who wanted to know how long she was going to flake off in bed. "Can we meet in the lounge?"

"Sure. One on the dot. Let's go back to Casa Bique. Last time I was here they had a stunning silver cigarette box. It cost an arm and a leg, but I should have bought it. If it's still there I will."

"As I remember, it had a stiff price tag. Just under a hundred, wasn't it?"

"About that."

"You'll have a hard time writing it off for ten dollars at Customs."

"I'll manage it, never fear."

The staff at the Hotel Fenix, like hotel staffs all over the world, were friendly and cooperative with airline crews. In exchange for a few civilities such as liquor for the manager and cigarettes for the clerks, they dispensed small courtesies and tips on new restaurants, what good films or shows were available, where the best buys were in the shops. There was small talk at the desk for a quarter of an hour and then the girls went up to their rooms.

Kelly, being a head stewardess, drew a single. It was early in the season, but Madrid was dry and hot. Fortunately, all first class Spanish hotels had air conditioning. Kelly undressed and crept into bed in the white-stippled room with the beautiful, dark, ornate furnishings. Spain had low rates and first-class accomodations. It was a beautiful, luxurious room.

Her alarm clock, set for twelve-thirty, ticked softly on the bedside table. It didn't bother her; it was familiar and cozy. She was asleep almost immediately.

• • •

A scream sounded somewhere. Trouble. There was trouble. The engines didn't sound right. There was that slight, almost imperceptible difference in the sound of the engines…

Someone was screaming.

We're in trouble, Kelly thought, and gathered herself together. It was just that she was pinned down…under something heavy. But I have to get out of here. I'm in charge, she told herself. Norm?

She said it frantically. "Listen, Norm, you have to get me out of here…"

"Captain!"

She struggled. *Get me out of here…*

She woke suddenly, breathing rapidly. The telephone was ringing, loud and clear.

It was only the telephone.

Dear God, I'm eating it and sleeping it and dreaming it, she thought, sliding out of bed. Job jitters had her down.

"Yes, hello," she said, at the phone. *"Quien?"*

The voice that answered was a man's. It was croupy, quavering and familiar. *"Si,* it is Senor Nascimento," the voice said. "This is the young lady from the plane? Senorita…Senorita Jones?"

"Yes."

"I am so sorry," he said. "Please forgive me."

"Not at all."

She turned and looked at her bedside clock. She'd slept for only half an hour. Half an hour, damn it. She could feel exhaustion in every muscle, every bone. What in the world did the man want? And how had he known where to reach her?

Frig it, she said silently and viciously. They didn't even let you sleep when the flight was over.

"I am so sorry to disturb you," the croupy voice apologized. He sounded agitated. "There have been difficulties. You understand… only that…because of these difficulties…how shall I say? Tsk tsk." He clucked impatiently, suddenly faced with linguistic troubles out of sheer excitement.

"What difficulties?" She spoke slowly, as to a child. "What is wrong, sir?"

He cleared his throat and made an obvious effort to master his discomposure. "Yes, difficulties," he echoed after her. "What difficulties? It is the boy, that Ricardo. He has disappeared."

The fog abruptly left Kelly's brain. "You mean he's *lost?*"

"No, the bag is lost."

"The…bag?"

"The bag of my wife. Where she has her *lana*. Her wool. The knitting, you understand."

"But what about Richard?"

"With the bag," he said simply. "Disappeared with the bag."

"Disappeared where?"

"Ah, if I knew that, then there would be no difficulty."

"But I don't understand. Didn't his people meet him?"

"So we were told," the Senor said, his voice crouping up badly. "When we inquired, we were told that someone had come for him, that he was gone. It was at the *aduana*. We were delayed there."

"You mean you got separated from Richard? But was he picked up all right? I mean, you don't suppose he's in any trouble, do you?"

"No, certainly not. Only we were separated and he is gone, like the wind, with the bag."

"But it was only knitting, wasn't it?" She tried to keep irritation out of her voice. They were old, they were good, they were kind.

But did she have to lose precious sleep because of a few hanks of wool?

"Ah," he laughed deprecatingly. "The pearls, you see. My wife's pearls. They were in the bag."

"Oh." Oh, she thought, and remembered the size of the pearls, the length of the strand. So they were real after all. But she had been sure of that. Her trips to the Orient had acquainted her with the value of jewels, especially pearls, and she had sized up the strand Senora Nascimento wore around her neck.

She shifted, reevaluating the Nascimentos. The picture coalesced in her mind. Why, they had thought it out very carefully, those two. The Senora had bought fine pearls in New York, probably at Tiffany's or Cartier's, where there would be little likelihood of an informer...no real danger of a chit sent to Madrid. The Senora had worn the pearls and then at the last minute had gotten cold feet.

"I think she broke them herself," Richard had said.

Undoubtedly she had. If caught, there would be only five percent on unstrung pearls...thirty-three percent if they were strung.

And then, to lessen the chances of being caught with the pearls, she had stuck them in her knitting bag, hidden in the hanks of wool, and had the child carry it for her. She probably would have gotten away with it.

Only Richard had absent-mindedly gone off with whoever called for him, with the bag still over his arm.

"Please?" the Senor said in her ear, very croupy indeed.

For a minute she was really disgusted. Then she remembered the things they all pulled. Lucille, with her costly silver cigarette box from the Casa Bique that she would manage to smuggle in. It wasn't murder, after all. The Nascimentos were no worse than plenty of others...and apparently no better, either.

It was really more in the nature of a disappointment. Those proud El Greco faces.

"Yes, Senor. Let me think. There must be something we can do. Of course, don't you imagine the boy will see to it that the bag is returned to you?"

"But how? Where would he look for us?"

"Certainly you're in the telephone book."

"*Que?*"

"In the—"

"*Si, si*…yes, certainly. But he may forget. Young children do not understand about these matters."

"I really don't think he'll forget. He seemed very fond of you and your wife. He'll get in touch with you. You found me easily enough. How *did* you locate me?"

"Through the office of the airline. Yes, of course. But he is such a young boy…and he may lose…he may be careless."

She resigned herself. The sooner she solved the Nascimento's problems the sooner she could go back to sleep. "I'll call the airport," she said crisply. "If your bag has been turned in you can take it from there. If not, I'll have them notify me if it's turned in later today. I'll get in touch with you one way or the other."

"Ah, thank you, Senorita. You think it will be returned?"

"I'm almost sure it will."

"*Gracias.* So much trouble, *si?* Oh, where you can reach us. Here is the number."

She wrote down the number on Hotel Fenix stationery. "No trouble at all," she said, cutting short his profuse thanks, and when she had hung up put through a telephone call to the airport. Waiting, she looked yearningly at the bed. And in the end the call was not fruitful. No petit point knitting bag "with roses and violets…about twelve by fourteen inches…" had been received by the claim office.

Would they let her know, please, if such a bag was in their possession within the next day or so? She was an employee of ITA and she was doing a service for one of the passengers on this morning's flight from New York.

Yes, they would let her know.

She lit a cigarette impatiently. Why did this little problem have to land in *her* lap? Since she had suggested it, surely Senor Nascimento could have contacted the field. There was only one valid explanation, namely that the Spanish couple had pulled a swindle at Customs and didn't wish to be involved as long as there was someone else to do their spade work for them.

It was, of course, an everyday occurrence. She had been told stories by Customs Inspectors. And they had been very clever, those two, using a young boy as a decoy.

But unfortunately for them, their plan had backfired.

What do you suppose they'd do now?

She picked up the piece of paper with the number Senor Nascimento had given her, took the receiver off the hook and then put it right back again. The hell, let them squirm. She went back to bed again. And had just settled between the covers when the phone rang once more.

She swore under her breath. Of course it was the Spanish couple. "Ring her, ring her," she could imagine the Senora saying, plucking at her husband's sleeve. "We must get back the pearls."

She slid out of bed and stalked over to the phone.

"Hello, hello," she said shortly. "Yes, what is it?"

But it wasn't the Senor. It was Miguel at the desk.

"Senorita Kelly?"

"Yes, Miguel."

"You have a visitor."

She sighed. "Who is it?"

"Quienes?" There was a chuckle and then he said, *"Pronto."*

Another voice came on the line. A very youthful voice.

"Kelly? It's I, Richard."

"Richard? Richard! Have you got the bag?"

"Yes, that's what it's all *about*," he said.

"But what happened? And how did you find me?"

"I had a bit of a time," he confessed. "I doubted you'd be at the Ritz, and you weren't. Then I tried the Palace. After that the Plaza and after this I was going to call the Wellington. But I was in luck, wasn't I?"

"Come on up," she said. "Tell the boy to get you to my room."

"Righto," he said, and rang off.

Twenty-four hours a day, that's what this job means, Kelly thought, but just the same she couldn't help being glad to see precocious Richard again. She got into a robe and waited for him. When the knock came at the door and she saw him standing outside, with that shock of blond hair falling into his eyes, she was ridiculously pleased.

"I don't usually entertain gentlemen in my room," she said. "But come in. I'll make an exception in your case."

He breezed in, carrying the familiar petit point bag in one hand, and sat down. "This is some hot climate," he observed. "Wouldn't it be stinking without air conditioning?" He fanned himself. "I've been under rather a strain," he confessed. "Here's Senora Nascimento's knitting bag. I thought you'd be the best one to get it to her."

He looked at the rumpled bed. "Oh, you've been taking a nap."

"I've been trying to," she said tartly. "With little success. First I had a telephone call from Senor Nascimento, saying that his wife's property was gone with the wind, and then you called. What in the world happened at the airport?"

"The damn chauffeur dragged me away. He wouldn't let me wait. I put up a holler but it didn't do any good. The Nascimentos were in a long line at Customs. The chauffeur is a first class crud. Jabbering a lot of this incomprehensible Spanish and I couldn't make him understand English. I didn't even get a chance to say good-bye to them. Or thank her. That stupid servant shoved me in the car and it was all very infuriating."

He added, simply, "She must think I'm buggo. And extremely impolite. Walking away with her stuff and then not even saying so long. Anyway. Will you return this, please?"

"Yes. Of course I will. It's just such an unforeseen thing to happen, that's all. I'm supposed to be on vacation. But I suppose I might have known *something* would happen."

She was vexed. Because I'm tired, she thought. After all, this was only another complication in a long string of complexities that made up an airline employee's life. She ought to be able to cope by now.

Richard must have sensed her displeasure. "It meant a lot of trouble and effort for me," he said. "But she was making that pink wooly thing and I knew she'd want to get on with it. Mostly, I regret leaving without—"

"Never mind, Richard, I'll get it back."

"And would you tell them I'd like to see them again?"

"All right, I will. How did you get over to the hotel? The chauffeur?"

"No, I took a taxi."

"I'll have one take you back. Meanwhile, you do look a little bushed. I'll order up something to drink. How about a coke?"

"Sure." His face brightened.

She called down for room service.

"I hope it won't take too long," he said anxiously. "I'm supposed to be taking a nap too, only I snuck out." He looked around. "You seem to be quite comfortable here."

"Yes, it's a good hotel. I've always liked it."

"Is that a balcony?"

"Yes, come on out and I'll show you a Gaudi house."

"What's that?"

"Follow me and I'll explain."

When they went outside she pointed to a building with a peaked roof and irregular architectural lines which were unorthodox in the extreme.

"That's a funny-looking thing," Richard commented. "It looks like Hansl and Gretl…the house in the forest."

"It does, sort of. You'll see more of them in Barcelona, if you go there. There are only one or two Gaudi houses in Madrid. He was an Art Nouveau architect, with some very wild ideas."

She looked across at the neighboring structure. "Yes, it's funny-looking. But it has a certain…"

She searched for the right word.

"You mean *panache*," Richard said officiously.

Yes, of course she had meant *panache*. Heavens, this kid was smart, she thought. She felt a little silly. "Um, that's right," she said, trying not to stare at him. After all, how many ten year old children knew a word like that?

"Shall we have our drinks out here?" she asked him.

"I guess not. I'm overheated. I'd sooner go inside where it's cool. Thank you, though."

The drinks came and Richard ignored the tall glass filled with cracked ice. He tilted his head and drank from the bottle.

"Taste good?"

"Groovy." He stuck his legs out and slid down on his spine. "Do you like Spain, Kelly?"

"Not as much as France or Italy. It's interesting, though. How do you feel about it?"

"I don't know yet. It's my first time here. I've been lots of places, but not here."

"Oh, you've done some other traveling, then?"

"Certainly." He looked a little offended. "I s'pose I know France the best. I've been to Paris," he said, folding down one finger. "And the Loire country." Another finger went down. "And the Provence." Three fingers were tucked under his thumb, and then a fourth joined them.

"And of course the Riviera," he said, jadedly.

"Oh, my."

"I don't know Italy *quite* as well. Rome, Florence, Milano. But just hurriedly. Of course at that time I was just a child."

She regarded him with amused tenderness. Here was this infant, barely ten years old, talking about a time when he was a *child.* He was really a dear little boy. "I was in Umbria," he said solemnly. "The Italian hill towns, where St. Francis walked…the musician of God. I remember it fairly well."

"It's beautiful country. You're a fortunate boy, Richard."

"I guess so." His gaze was watchful, as if he suspected her of condescending.

"But you are. Me too. There are people who never get to see the world, who always stay a few yards from where they were born, more or less."

"Yeah, I guess so. Probably."

"Where are you staying in Madrid?"

"With Uncle Constant."

"Oh?"

"He's quite a pleasant person. Though I must say I don't really dig his wife."

"His wife?"

"Dolores. His second wife. Of course she's very *pretty.* She's, you know, about as young as you are. Whereas my uncle is old, like my father. Dolores looks like a marble statue. Or maybe a painting. You know…Tintoretto. Like that."

"I see," she said dryly. "Tintoretto. Like that."

"Anyway, a Renaissance type. Marvelous bone structure."

"Really?"

She was dazed. This prodigy would get his PH D at the age of sixteen, she thought. Was there anything he didn't know?

He took another swig of his Coca Cola, then put the bottle down on top of the desk. "My aunt is a good friend of mine," he volunteered.

"You mean Dolores?"

"No no. My real aunt. Before they got a divorce."

"Got a…are you talking about your uncle's first wife?"

"Yes, Aunt Elizabeth. I've always been rather a favorite of hers. She's not spectacular looking but she's…well, very kind."

He hefted the coke bottle again and drank, not too quietly. Then he set it down again and shrugged. "I feel so sorry for her," he said. "Though of course she's well taken care of. Financially, I mean."

"Does she live in New York too?"

"Uh huh. She doesn't have a husband now. I don't think she wants one."

"I see."

"Dolores has beautiful clothes. But I think she's shallow. Quite a bit like my own—"

He stopped short and flushed.

Kelly started to ask whom he meant to compare Dolores Comstock with and then, in a flash, it came to her. Why, he was thinking of his own mother!

She looked at him for a moment and then looked away again. Poor little rich boy, she thought. Nobody to love him and nobody to love. With the possible exception of Aunt Elizabeth, his Uncle Constant's discarded wife.

She was casual about it. "Anyway, this is a nice holiday for you, to visit your relatives in Madrid."

He yawned. "I don't know exactly what I'm going to do with myself, but I suppose I can find something."

The yawn was a front. The elaborately offhand manner in which he phrased his worry about the bleak prospect of being cooped up with a busy uncle and an indifferent aunt was also a front. Kelly said, "Why, certainly they'll see that you meet some young people your own age."

"It isn't likely," he said, and drank some more coke.

"Why not? Else your parents wouldn't have sent you here. They want you to have a good time. Isn't that so?"

"It was my uncle's decision to have me here."

"What do you mean?"

"Daddy's away. In Afghanistan. He's a financier. He's always off somewhere. It's generally a problem to know what to do with me after school closes."

"What about your mother? Didn't she want to have you with them in…Afghanistan, you said?"

"Oh, no, Mummy's not there. She's in…I *think* she's in Rome."

He put down his empty coke bottle and stood up.

"It was nice seeing you again."

"Wait…"

She got up too. "Listen, you wouldn't be free for dinner tonight, would you?"

"For dinner? Why?"

"If you were, I'd ask you to dine with me."

"You would? Then I'm free." His eyes glistened. "You just have to ring my uncle and explain who you are, then you'll probably be permitted to call round for me. I'll tell him you're going to ask for my company."

"Can I phone now? While you're here?"

"No, I'm supposed to be resting. And I have to hurry back to bed before I'm found out." He looked around. "Can I have something to write on, the address and stuff?"

She gave him a piece of hotel notepaper. He scribbled on it and then she took a look at it. "Is your uncle in the diplomatic service, Richard?"

"Yes. He's an air attache for the U.S. Government. He started out as a Lieutenant in the Armed Forces. And he had some flying background in the Korean War, which should interest you, Kelly. Then he was an aide to a General, who got him appointed to Spain."

Kelly hid a smile. "You seem to have a full dossier on your uncle, Richard."

"I believe in finding things out about people. Besides, I've heard a hundred times about him, from my aunt." He glanced up at her. "Why did you ask if he was in the diplomatic service?"

"Because that's a section where many of them live. Well, fine then, Richard, it's a date for tonight. I'll wait half an hour or so, then I'll call there."

"Okay. And now I hafta go."

"Just a second, I'm going to call downstairs and have the desk clerk get you a taxi."

He stood on one foot while she dialed Miguel. "See that my young friend gets transportation back to his home," she told the clerk, and when she was assured it would be taken care of Richard hurried out and Kelly went to the phone again, to tell Senor Nascimento about the return of the bag.

Another voice answered, but almost instantly the Senor was speaking. He must have been sitting by the phone, and he went into raptures when he heard the good news. He would be forever in her debt. "Richard thought it would be nice to see you again," she said. "I thought maybe we could drop the bag off at your home."

"No no no," he said quickly. "Thank you so very much, but I could not put you to all that trouble." He didn't say a word about Richard, but hurriedly suggested that she leave the bag at the desk of her hotel.

"Very well, Senor Nascimento. I'll have it downstairs right away."

Well, that was the end of that, thank God.

As soon as she put the phone down it rang again. This time it was Lucille. "It's getting on toward one," she said. "How about it? You haven't conked out, have you?"

"No, I'll meet you as scheduled."

Lucille rang off and once more she rang for the desk.

"Miguel? Could you send a boy up. To pick up something that will be called for by a Senor Nascimento."

"*Si*, okay," he said, and in less than five minutes a boy knocked at the door.

"Please take this to the desk and give it to Miguel. *Gracias*." She fished in her handbag and dug out a couple of pesetas.

Then, when she was alone again, she ran a bath, sat in the warm, soapy water until she felt very relaxed and pleased with life in general, after which she dried herself and got dressed again. She locked the door of her room and went downstairs. And then remembered that she had to call Richard's uncle. Miguel rang for her, but she didn't speak to Uncle Constant. After a few words with some servant whose English was none too good she was turned over to Richard's stepaunt.

Dolores Comstock was, unexpectedly, Spanish. She had a rich, throaty voice with an accent that was thick enough to cut with a knife.

Dolores…

She should have realized. It was a name as Spanish as Carmen.

"I'm sorry to call unexpectedly like this," Kelly said. "But I'm with the airline that brought your nephew over. I thought—"

There was a quick interruption. "Richard? He is not my nephew, in point of fact. He is my husband's nephew."

"Oh yes, I see."

"Anyway, excuse me. What is this about the child?"

"I wondered if I could take him to dinner tonight."

There was a little silence. Then, "Are you there?" the voice asked. "I am sorry, I dropped the phone. Someone is doing my hair and another girl is attending to my nails. Are you there?"

"Yes, Mrs. Comstock."

"You want to take the little boy to dinner?" Genuine astonishment. "Why?"

"Because I grew rather fond of him."

Sounds from the background. Muted voices. Kelly pictured the scene…a pampered woman, in the hands of solicitous beauty operators. She waited, half-amused, half-bored, until the voice came on again.

"Aren't you nice." Mrs. Comstock said, in that melting accent. "Will you be careful of him? My husband is worried about the child." She became very conversational. "There is some family trouble, you understand. He is neglected, no? I know that my husband went to some trouble to get him over here. You see—"

There was another pause, during which Kelly distinctly heard the word *"mierda"* which, in Spanish, meant the same thing as the French *"merde"*. It was an earthy term not used in the best society. There was then a quick spate of Spanish in the background. What now? Kelly wondered. A too tight roller? A slight slash of the cuticle? And then, making little sounds of annoyance, the woman spoke into the phone again.

"*Perdon*…excuse me," she apologized. "These people are so careless. Forgive me. Just a little question, you understand. How do I know you are who you say you are?"

"I always carry all my credentials," Kelly said calmly. "But of course if you would rather not have me take Richard for the evening, I will certainly understand."

"Oh, if you have your credentials," Mrs. Comstock said gaily, "then I am sure it will be all right. As a matter of fact, my husband will not be home until very late, and I am scheduled for a dinner party this evening. What did you say your name was?"

How did I get into this? she thought.

"Kelly Jones."

The name was painstakingly repeated.

"Is it settled, then, Mrs. Comstock?"

"Yes, my dear. You are very thoughtful. Of course Richard will have money. I couldn't let you go to that expense."

"You can give Richard money if you like," Kelly said pleasantly, though inclined to boil inside. "But I'm taking your nephew—that is, your husband's nephew—to dinner. Forgive me, but it's my pleasure."

There was a small explosion of laughter. "You sound like *very* fun," the other woman said delightedly. "We must get to know each other. You're pretty, I suppose. All of those girls are pretty. My husband will like you very much. He adores pretty girls. You know that a good wife is not a possessive one, so I won't mind if he…maybe I'll see you tomorrow, *si?*"

"Why, thank you."

"Anyway, my dear, have a pleasant evening."

"I thought I'd call round for Richard at about eight o'clock."

"Yes, very good."

There was a quick good-bye and then the phone was hung up.

It was while she was on the phone arranging about Richard that she saw the name on the register on top of the desk. The book was opened to the day's listings and of course it was turned the opposite way. It was the bold, dark scrawl that caught her eye among all the other indifferent hen scratchings that ran across the lined page. Idly reading upside down, she made out the first name…Steven…and reached out to swivel the book round.

Steven Connaught.

Miguel saw her looking at it. *"Que?"* he asked, smiling.

She put a finger next to the name. "He was on my flight coming over."

"Good-looking. Spends, too. The best cigars. And big tips."

The Hotel Fenix had a splendid flight of stairs, baroque and crimson-carpeted. At that precise moment, while they were discussing him, Mr. Connaught came down the steps. Kelly hastily pushed aside the register and Miguel hid a grin.

"Imagine seeing you again so soon," Steve Connaught said in that deep, rumbling drawl. "So this is where you girls put up."

"Sometimes. Most times."

"You look fresh and rested."

"I had some sleep."

"I had a little too." He looked her over. It was thorough but not really offensive. It was just that for some reason she was vulnerable with this man. He was so extraordinarily—

Attractive.

She found herself, for example, chattering like an idiot.

"As I said, I had *some* sleep. But it wasn't very…well, I thought I'd rest for hours, but…you see, the telephone kept ringing. I was getting in and out of bed…"

She broke off. He had finished his inspection of her and when his eyes met hers again they were quietly approving. "If you don't have a rule about going out with strangers," he said, "I'd like it if I could take you to dinner. I think I introduced myself on the plane, but in case it went in one ear and out the other, my name's Steve Connaught. Yours, as I recall, is Kelly something or other."

"Kelly Jones."

He held out his hand once more, as he had on the plane. There was no undue pressure of his fingers, just a firm handclasp. "Would it be on for that dinner?" he asked, and Kelly had the impression that when she said no, there would be nothing held against her and no skin, for that matter, off his nose.

Yet she would have given a lot to be able to say yes.

Only there was the little matter of Richard Comstock. The poor, lonely little rich boy. I had to be the do-gooder, she thought. I had to sew up my evening.

"I'm sorry," she said. "I'd really like to, but I've already promised to spend the evening with someone."

He smiled briefly. "Have a good time anyway."

"Thanks. I'm taking the unaccompanied minor to Botin's."

"The who...what?"

"Richard Comstock. The little boy on the flight over."

"No kidding."

"He seems to be rather tossed about by...well, family. But he did someone a very nice favor. So I'm taking him out for the evening."

"How about making it a threesome?"

"Oh, but—"

"Be fine with me if it's all right with you."

"Well, surely. Yes, all right, thanks very much."

"Good. Meet me in the lounge for a drink first? Seven?"

"Yes, fine."

"Until then," he said and, nodding, moved on and out the front doors.

"Good-looking," Miguel repeated, smirking conspiratorially. *"Muy simpatico."*

"I'm a little afraid of him."

"Why? You have a chaperon, the boy. Nothing to be afraid of."

"I didn't mean that, exactly."

"Then what?"

"I don't know."

She went into the lounge. Lucille was on her second brandy. She was a little high. "I've been waiting," she complained. "What have you been doing?"

"Resting," Kelly said ironically, and they went out together into the bright Madrid sunshine.

CHAPTER 3

The Casa Bique, a stately old mansion hidden behind immense trees, had an American management and so did not observe siesta. The interior was cool, due to its thick stone walls, and the girls wandered through the high-ceilinged rooms, selecting, rejecting, and finally settling on a few objects that were too glittering to resist. Lucille's silver cigarette box was, fortunately, still unsold.

"I'll stick it in my make-up kit," she said to Kelly. "No one will be the wiser."

Both of them bought gifts, and some things for themselves as well. Totalled, their purchases came to about a thousand pesetas, or just over three hundred dollars.

This haul would enter the U.S. undeclared. Somehow, each of them would find a way to get the stuff in without paying duty. And again Kelly thought, we're all venal at bottom. She had never really dwelt on it before, but thinking now about the volume of illicit traffic in small and large items, she was a little ashamed. It was not that she was Establishment; it was more that, after her many forays abroad, with treasures she had slipped in from other countries to her own, she thought now that it was no more unworthy to smuggle priceless things than it was more modest purchases.

Where did you draw the line?

Later, they walked a bit and then had a *tonica* at an outdoor cafe on the Plaza de Cibeles. Kelly sipped her drink and said suddenly, "Lucille…"

"Yes?"

"We're friends, right?"

"I've always thought so. What's the pitch?"

"Would you do a big favor for me?"

"Sure."

"I have something I don't want to declare. Would you put it in your bra on your return trip?"

"Good heavens. Okay. Will it fit?"

"Yes. And then, darling, leave it off at the apartment for me. All right?"

"Sure. No trouble at all."

"It's just a little hash."

"*What?*"

"You don't mind?"

"Who are you carrying hash for?"

"Does it matter?"

"No, of course not," Lucille said hastily. "It's your business."

But she was glad to see a reserved look in the other girl's eye. "You're not keen about doing it, are you?"

There was a little silence. "Well, I—" Lucille shrugged. "I just didn't figure you for—"

"Okay, I was only making funnies."

The other girl gave her a long look. "What led up to this?" she finally asked.

Kelly picked up her glass, with the slice of lemon at the bottom. "Forget it. I don't have anything for you to sneak in. It was just…a train of thought."

"But what started it?"

"Some people on the plane. I just suddenly started thinking about how hard it must be for Customs. That they must have one hell of a problem with…people beating the rap."

Lucille's bright face, topped by her blond, cropped hairdo, was questioning. "Are you suffering from fatigue syndrome?" she asked sympathetically.

"Maybe. No. Not really." Kelly, surrounded by sunshine and sheltering palm trees, shaded in a quiet oasis on a beautiful avenida in Madrid, laughed. "File it away in a corner of your mind and for the moment stop thinking about it. It may mean something some day. But for now, allow as how I didn't say anything."

"You mean I should pay duty on what I bought today?" Lucille asked, astonished.

"No, silly. Don't give it another thought. I just have a funny feeling."

"About what?"

"I'm not sure. But I think I've stumbled on to something. It's just a feeling. God, it's hot. Catch that waiter's eye, if you can. I could go for another *tonica*."

• • •

After siesta they went to the Gran Via, window-shopped and picked up a few minor items, then returned to the hotel where a party was in progress in a stewardess's room. It was just the girls, and they were going fairly light on the liquor but definitely bypassing rules by drinking at all so soon before flight time, which was only a few hours away. But of course Kelly wasn't in danger at the moment, since she was not returning with them, and they knew she wouldn't spill things to the Captain in command.

It was shortly before six when the girls changed into their uniforms and settled their caps on their heads. "You with your twelve days off," Lucille said, saying good-bye. "Nobody deserves it more."

They all went off with their loot, tipping on the way, and then Kelly went to her own room. It's a funny life, she thought, sitting on the edge of the bed. Nice…but driftless.

If it hadn't been for the thought of the evening ahead, she would have felt lost, and lonely. Suddenly, with them all gone, everything seemed so terribly quiet.

Damn it, can't you ever relax? she asked herself angrily.

At a few minutes past seven Kelly locked her room from the outside and was just about to go down the hall when she heard the ringing of the telephone inside.

Should she answer that?

When it kept on ringing she unlocked the door again. It was Senor Nascimento.

"Yes, hello," she said, trying not to sound rushed.

"It's terrible," he said. "I can't…Senorita, I don't know what could have happened!"

"Didn't you get the bag?"

"Yes. Thank you, *gracias*, but oh, my goodness—"

"What's the trouble?"

"An unforeseen development! I called for the bag, at your hotel. Thank you, Senorita. Only when I reached home there was something missing."

"Missing? Well, what?"

"My wife's beads."

"Your wife's—"

"You know, the pearls," he said, his voice dropping. "They were not in the bag."

Oh, for heaven's sake, she thought. Why did I *answer*?

"I'm so sorry, but I don't know anything about it," she said rapidly. "And Senor Nascimento, I'm in rather a hurry. Could I call you back tomorrow?"

"Tomorrow?" He sounded shocked. "But what about *now*? What about…" He wheezed. "Something must be done *now*."

"What would you suggest, sir?"

There was a breathless pause, and then he came on again. "You must realize that it is a great disaster, Senorita. Can't you—"

"I'm really very sorry," she said implacably. "But I'm already late for an appointment."

This time the man's voice was shrill. "But I don't understand," he cried. "You see, there were the beads. Well, not very expensive beads but my wife is—"

"Senor Nascimento," she said, hanging on to the last shreds of her patience, "I can't help you at the moment. I have to meet someone."

"Just the same," he said desperately, "we have something missing, Senorita! You must comprehend! It is very difficult! My wife and I…we bought some valuable pearls. You must know how it is. Investments…everyone does it. My God, Senorita, they are gone! They were in the bag but they are not in there now…"

"I'm sorry," she said. "I don't know anything about it. Believe me, I can understand how you feel. But I'm already late for an appointment. You must let me call you at another time."

"No no, we must get this straightened out now…because it is of the utmost importance. Senorita?" His voice went up an octave.

"Forgive me," she said. "I must go now."

And above his frantic protestations, she hung up.

What was it all about? At the moment she didn't care. I'll worry about it tomorrow, she thought, and taking a last careful look in the mirror, she left the room again and went downstairs. She left the key at the desk, with Miguel, and walked into the lounge. Steve Connaught was there, near a window. The late afternoon light gilded the table top, streamed gloriously through the violet and crimson leaded panes. There was a bowl of dried flowers, soft beige mixed with a harsher red, in the center of the table. There were about a dozen persons in the room; a mixture of English, Spanish and French assailed Kelly's ears.

"Hello," Steve said, and rose.

"Hello."

"You're only twenty minutes late," he said pleasantly.

"I'm late because people insist on ringing my telephone with insoluble problems."

"How so?"

"For one, the Nascimentos. You remember the Spanish couple on the plane?"

"The ones who kept the little boy occupied?"

"Yes. I've had quite a day. They've called me twice."

"What about?"

"First, to let me know that Richard went off with the Senora's knitting bag."

"He did?"

"Yes. Apparently the Nascimentos were delayed at Customs. Richard had this bag belonging to them. When they got off the line Richard had disappeared."

"With the bag."

"With the bag. The next call I had was from Richard. He was in the lobby, with the knitting bag."

"You did have quite a day."

"There's more to it."

"Tell me."

"Oh…on the plane Richard managed to break the Senora's string of pearls."

"Yes, I remember. Everyone was on hands and knees."

"And then when they were all collected and accounted for, the Senora stuffed them into her knitting bag. Can you conjecture?"

He looked at her. "The pearls were expensive?"

"Yes, I had a good look at them."

"You think they were purchased outside of Spain."

"I think it's a safe guess."

"Happens all the time," he said. "Are you worrying about it?"

"Not in the least. I wouldn't have given it a second thought if it hadn't been for one thing."

"What's that?"

"I left the bag at the desk, and Senor Nascimento was to call round for it. I had a pleasant afternoon, shopping with a friend, and just as I was about to come downstairs to meet you, the telephone rang again."

"And?"

"It was Senor Nascimento once more. He had picked up the bag, but there was something missing."

"Not the pearls."

"Oh, but yes."

"What could have happened?"

"I have no idea. I didn't think to look in the bag. It's just another nagging, troublesome *je ne sais quoi* in the life of an airline employee. May I have a martini?"

"Straight up or on the rocks?" he asked, signalling the waiter.

"Up."

When the drink came she asked him how he had spent his own time. "I sightsaw," he said. "Mainly, the Prado."

"Nice place."

He looked discontented. "The lighting's bad. The Michelangelos on the staircase, for one thing. Sisyphus…you have to stand on your head, practically. But of course the Goyas and the Velasquez rooms were all right, and they were my chief interest."

"Have you been to Madrid before?"

"This is my first visit to Spain."

"Madrid's a stately city. Do you like it?"

"Very much, what I've seen. I thought about going to Barcelona first, but that can wait."

"Barcelona's all right. Raffish. A seaport city. I'm not too partial to it. The Estoril, of course, is beautiful."

"When are you returning to New York?" he asked.

"Not for a while. I have some time off. In a few days I'll take off for Malaga. Drive through Andalusia. I've never done that."

"Sounds nice."

"Yes, I think I'll enjoy it."

"When are you leaving?"

"I'm booked for a Wednesday flight at ten in the morning."

"I see."

"And where are you going next, Mr. Connaught?"

"I haven't decided."

He picked up his glass again. "I usually manage to work in Paris, whatever else I do. So as usual, I suppose I'll end up there."

"It happens to be my favorite city."

"Does it?" He gave her a long, assessing look. "Then we seem to be on the same wave length. It's mine too, that is, in Europe."

And soon they were comparing impressions. "Montmartre in the evening, the Ile St. Louis by day," Steve said.

"I love the Quai des Augustins, with the antique shops."

"And the Pont Neuf…ever been to La Reine Jeanne, just across the bridge from the parvis of Notre Dame?"

"A restaurant?"

"One of the best."

He told her about it. "A bistro, but the best Coquille St. Jacques you ever tasted. A Coq au Vin you wouldn't believe. The Pot au Feu…"

"I must remember it."

"Go there, you won't be sorry." He cut the tip of a cigar and lit it. "Well, there's Europe, which admittedly is an enchanted continent. But my heart belongs to Vermont."

"Vermont?"

She couldn't have been more astonished. Steve Connaught was Tangiers and Marrakesh. You could picture him in Greece, among the bitter lemons, or at Rapallo, on a terrace overlooking the sea. But in New England?

"You come from Vermont?"

"Oh, no." He leaned back, exhaling smoke. "I was born in Brooklyn."

It was even more outlandish. "I don't believe it," she said.

"Oh? Must I remind you that Brooklyn has yielded some of the best talent of the century?" There was a slow grin. "When you spit on Brooklyn, spit with a smile."

"I wasn't spitting on it. It's just…surprising."

"It's got a cachet of its own. I've been told that when the Americans liberated Paris, they did a good selling job on Brooklyn. The whole damned infantry came from there. In the movie houses, every time Brooklyn was mentioned in a film, the G.I.'s clapped and cheered." His grin widened. "After they left, the French audiences carried on the tradition. Brooklyn? Everyone snickers; I've never known why. That crazy place has something. Damned if I know what it is. But it's there. Maybe it's the last stronghold of Americana. In some nutty way."

"Three cheers for Brooklyn," Kelly said. "A ho and a ho and a ho." She leaned forward. Maybe it was only to claim his attention, because Connaught, even in the midst of a conversation, had a tendency to rove the room with his eyes. Is he with me or not? Kelly kept wondering, as his glance strayed to this person and then that. Or maybe it was because she liked the smell of his shaving lotion. She moved her chair forward a little. "All right, Brooklyn," she said. "Now what's this about Vermont?"

"Heaven on earth," he said. "Highest suicide rate in the nation."

"You do pique a person's interest. First it's heaven on earth and then it's the place where suicide occurs oftenest."

"Oh, it's lonely," he said. "Lonely as hell. Cold most of the time so that when the spring thaw comes, you think of Strindberg. You know? Where Elis says, 'The double windows have been taken down and fresh curtains put up…yes, its spring again…' "

She stared at him. Strindberg? How were you supposed to tag this man? Looked like C.I.A. or even Mafia. And then he quoted from a playwright who was the darling of the intellectuals.

"I have a house there," he said abruptly. "Had it built the way I wanted it. I go there whenever I can find the time."

"Why aren't you there now?" she asked quickly.

"Because I'm here," he said flatly, and swivelled his eyes away from hers.

Was it meant for a laugh? She didn't know. But she laughed anyway. He himself didn't crack a smile. "What's your house like?" she asked.

"Nutty. I damn near had a duel with the architect. You can't do this, he kept saying. No one in his right mind wants six bathrooms for a four bedroom house. It was a fight to the finish, but I have my six bathrooms."

"It does seem a little out of Krafft Ebbing. What is it in your past that makes you love Johns?"

"Eight kids and one can," he said succinctly. "Satisfied?"

"Maybe I can understand that."

"I wonder." He gave her an almost hostile look. "You come from Greenwich, Connecticut and your parents had two kids, each with a room of their own, a nice room, with a toilet between you. You prepped at a good school, private, and you and your sister—or brother—never knew what it was like to be hungry."

His jaw jutted out aggressively. "Correct me if I'm wrong."

"It was Scarsdale," she murmured.

"Same difference."

"Are you an inverse snob, Mr. Connaught?"

There was a quick, wry smile. "Is this Mr. and Miss business going to go on all night?"

"Night" never had a more enticing sound. A little shiver ran through Kelly. To spend a night with this blunt, plain-speaking man…

"All right, Steve," she said.

"I'm not any kind of snob. And don't you be, either."

It was as if he had said, "No snobs in *this* family." It was intimate and…I'm getting way ahead of myself, she thought, and reminded herself that this was just a date with someone from her most recent flight.

He signaled the waiter. "What time are we calling for the… what was it you called him?"

"The unaccompanied minor. I said we'd be around there at about eight."

"That gives us plenty of time for another drink," he said, and asked for refreshers. After that they talked idly, until he looked at his watch and said it was just about time to get going. Did she want to powder her nose?

"No."

He gave her another one of those assessing looks. "That's fine. I don't like mirror-lookers much. Anyway, you have a face that doesn't need much working-over, I'd say."

"Thanks." Damn it, that sounded prim, she thought.

"That's all the compliments I'm going to pay you tonight," he said. "Have to save some for tomorrow."

As they walked through the open glass doors, he put his hand on her elbow and, at the first street crossing, pressed closer to her, so that his hand lightly—oh, very lightly, touched her breast. She had the feeling it wasn't even intentional. And when they had reached the other side, he let go of her arm, but the tingle of the contact remained. Spring surged through Kelly's veins, and the purple bougainvillea on the Avenida de la Castellana stabbed at her with its lush beauty. The center esplanade was studded with palms, imaginative and exotic. This was one of the most beautiful streets in the world.

She had explained that it was within walking distance, and they strolled leisurely. "It should be right about here," she said after a while. "Number 1400...I think the next one must be it."

•••

The Comstock house was on the Paseo de la Castellana, recessed from the broad avenida, with a front courtyard behind an iron gate. The building itself was almost concealed behind lush trees and planting. It was four stories high, a soft-white brick with beautiful embellishments and balconies.

"Pretty fancy," Steve commented, as they went up the tiled walk and climbed the four broad stone steps to the handsome doorway. He put a finger on the bell.

Waiting, he reached up and plucked a spray of purple flowers from an overhanging bush. "For you," he said, handing it to her. "It matches your eyes."

"Flattery will—" she started to say, and then the door opened. A rather pretty young girl in a crisp white uniform welcomed them in when they said who they were. She padded ahead of them, in some kind of soft slippers, and led them into a small *sala*. "Please wait, thank you," she said and then, with a shy, dimpled smile, left them.

Like all Spanish interiors, there was an immediate impression of repressed brightness; louvres were slatted at the windows, but the fugitive gold from outside shot in to make random patterns on the carpet. Greenery, in stone pots, and the inevitable purple bougainvillea massed in great bowls on table tops gave the room a hot-house atmosphere in spite of the very creditable air-conditioning, which seemed to be centrally-controlled.

Dim, mysterious, with the heavy, dark, carved furniture indigenous to Spanish rooms, it was a lovely salon in what was undoubtedly a magnificent house. The entrance hall through which they had passed had been stately and high-ceilinged, with a frescoed dome and splendidly tiled floors.

"Not bad," Steve said.

"It's lovely." She sat beside him, waiting. "I've walked down this street many an afternoon. I've always longed to see the inside of one of these houses."

"A dream realized," he drawled.

"In a way it is," she said, faintly irritated, which he sensed at once.

"I didn't mean to be cynical," he apologized. "I understand completely. In my own way, I'm a dreamer too."

They weren't alone for very long. There were footsteps on the tiled floor outside and then Richard walked chipperly into the room, with a woman behind him.

"Hi," he said, and saw Steve right away. "Oh, you were on the plane," he said. "You're the one who smokes the cigars."

"Any objection?"

"No! Gee, I didn't know there'd be three of us. But I think I have enough money for us all."

"Save your dough for bubble-gum," Steve said. "Tonight is my treat."

"It's very nice of you. I'm afraid I don't know your name."

"It's Steve Connaught."

Richard turned to his duenna. "These are my friends," he announced, and then introduced the woman. "This is Joia."

Joia. Did it mean "joy"? If so, the bent old woman was inaptly named. She was like a Kathe Kollwitz drawing, with eyes that looked burnt-out and bleak. Yet there was sweetness in back of them, and her hands on the child's shoulders were solicitous.

She nodded. "So, then. You will have a good time with these friends of yours."

"I sure will." His face was bright and expectant.

"Take care of him," the woman said simply, looking first at Kelly and then at Steve.

"Don't worry. We'll have him home at a reasonable hour."

"Thank you."

They went outside and there was now a limousine there, in the *port cochere*, with a strikingly handsome man of thirty odd wiping the tonneau with a soft cloth. He straightened up when they walked down the stone path, and Kelly had a glimpse of an olive-skinned, strong face with sepia eyes and a sensual mouth. His body, lithe and supple, was bare to the waist, revealing rippling muscles gleaming with sweat.

He saw Richard and put his hand up. His smile showed gleaming white teeth.

Richard's answering smile was perfunctory.

"That's the chauffeur," he volunteered and they gained the street, where Steve stood, with uplifted finger, intent on hailing a cruising cab.

After almost a quarter of an hour they snagged one. "About time," Steve said, as they got in. "I had no lunch at all, so I'm famished. And we have quite a distance to go, I understand."

"I had a lousy lunch," Richard said, not to be outdone. "Some kind of fishy soup, which made me want to vomit, so I'm hungry too. I don't really think I like Spanish food."

"You'll like it where we're going," Kelly promised, and at last they reached the Puerta del Sol, where Botin's was located in an ancient quarter of the city, The restaurant was two centuries old, one of the very special culinary landmarks of Madrid. Touristy, yes, but just the same authentic, historied, with one of the best cuisines in all Spain. Old-world, leaning not at all on elegance but instead on the excellence of its product, it was below street level and was labyrinthine, with its network of rooms and open kitchens.

The leaded glass panes next to the table at which the three of them were seated were violet and rose and umber in the last, dying light of the long, semi-tropical day. The cooking areas, behind glass, were alive with the brilliant blue tile so indigenous to Spain. Steam swirled round the white-capped chefs behind the windows; the aromas were mouth-watering.

"Keen," Richard said, looking around. "This place is keen." He leaned his elbows on the table. "I also dig having dinner at nine o'clock at night."

"Do you, darling? I hate it. It's my major complaint about Spain and Portugal. I get so annoyed with these dining rooms with the ropes up until nine-thirty or ten. Personally, I think it's barbaric."

"It's a way of life," Steve remarked.

"One that I'm not fond of. The irritating thing is that you can't find a place for a light lunch during the day. Everything is in courses."

"I'm inclined to agree," Steve said. "I never was a six course guy myself. Give me a good porterhouse with onions and an Idaho and a girlie show afterwards. That's my style."

"What's a girlie show?" Richard asked interestedly.

"Just talking off the cuff," Steve said gruffly. "I say a lot of things I don't really mean."

"Why?"

"Because I'm me, that's why. Big talker." He turned to Kelly. "Another drink?"

"I'll skip another drink. But you go ahead."

"No, I'll skip it too. Frankly, I'm dying to eat." He summoned the waiter, and after scanning their menus all three decided on the suckling pig.

There would be a half hour wait, they were told, and Steve suggested a tour of the place, so they got up and wandered off into other rooms. The clientele was in the main American and English, with the usual scattering of German tourists. However, crowded around the bar area there were some local residents, Madrid types from all classes. Workingmen were mixed with well-suited businessmen, and one or two women, with escorts, sat on stools.

A roving cameraman approached them. "Take your picture?"

"Uh uh," Steve said, turning his back, but Richard got quite excited. "Oh, can't we?" he asked. "Gee, Steve, I'd like that."

"Hell, it's such a sucker gimmick," Steve objected, but relented. The shutter clicked as the flash exploded. "Pronto…ten minutes," the photographer said and went looking for other easy marks.

Since they had to wait for dinner anyway, there was another drink at the bar, which had a little more color, and then they went back to their table again. Just before the meal arrived the photographer brought them the blown-up photos. It was not unflattering, Kelly saw, giving a quick look at herself. But Steve complained that he looked like a thug.

"Aren't you?" Kelly asked, feeling her drinks.

"What do you think?" he countered.

"I think maybe you are," she murmured, while Richard pored over the pictures of himself and his new friends.

"You may be right," Steve said, and that was all she could get out of him.

• • •

"It was good, but I can't swallow another mouthful," Steve said, pushing his plate back.

It was true. Half of their meal could have been taken home in a doggie bag. Only Richard wanted dessert. Kelly and Steve settled for coffee and a cognac. They sat and chatted, while a steady stream of people came through the doors. It was almost eleven o'clock, but that was Spain for you. A night country.

"I'm having a super time," Richard said. "I don't generally stay up this late." He caught himself up instantly, realizing his faux pas. Now, his upward glance at Kelly seemed to say, you'll decide I've been up past my bedtime.

"But I'm not a bit tired," he said quickly.

"All right, just a little bit longer," Kelly agreed, lacking moral fibre. She was a sucker for his round, childish face, his limpid blue eyes, his blond hair that swept down across his forehead. I'll undoubtedly be a very bad, over-permissive mother, she thought, and stuck a cigarette in her mouth brusquely. A porcine slob three tables back was eyeing her furtively; a distasteful type, occupied with picking the bones of a capon, his heavy-lidded eyes resting on her with avidity. He was all the nasty men she ran into all too often in her job, and she wished she were facing the opposite way.

Steve lit a cigar.

"I like the smell," Richard said. "*Your* cigars don't turn me off, Steve."

He pushed back his chair. "I have to find the bathroom, I suddenly realized."

"I'll go with you," Steve said, rising. "Hold the fort," he told Kelly. "We have to see a man about a dog."

"Cheero."

She sat there, over her cognac. She was perfectly happy…yes, that was the word. Of course it had to end, though one wished it didn't. She looked at the professional snapshot again. Steve, unsmiling and tight-jawed, looked like someone in a Rogues' Gallery. She gazed long at the grim, cheerless face. Why did women like questionable men? The answer was obvious. It was the unknown, the mysterious, that intrigued.

And yet he had quoted Strindberg.

Richard's beaming face looked back at her. A handsome boy. Her own smile, professional out of long habit. I do have nice hair, she thought. The face that looked back at her was like a stranger's all the same. Would you recognize yourself on the street? she had often wondered. You only saw yourself head-on, in a mirror. What does the back of you look like? How do you hold yourself? You spot friends walking along…but would you spot yourself?

We're not what we look like but what we feel like, she thought and then, after studying the three faces for several minutes her eye suddenly went beyond Richard, Steve and herself. In the background was the crowded bar…and suddenly there was a familiar profile. She knew that man.

Slowly, it came to her. It was the chauffeur she had seen, briefly, outside the *quinta* of Constant Comstock on the Paseo de la Castellana. That tall, muscled man with the bushy triangle of dark, strong hair on his chest.

It *was* that man.

She was almost sure of it.

And as she studied the faintly blurred, tall man in the background, she became certain that it was the Comstock driver. Surely that was the same face, the same eyes, the same splendid build? That sensual mouth…

Her next reaction was one of annoyance, anger perhaps. So the Comstocks were keeping an eye on Richard's companions. In spite of her credentials. They had assigned the houseman to monitor the evening.

What of it?

Just the same, she was coldly critical. And when Richard returned to the table, alone, she was hard put not to take out her displeasure on him. Yet how could she blame the boy for his family's distrust?

"Where's Steve?" she asked.

"Combing his hair. Or something. He made me comb mine too. He said we had to spruce ourselves up because we were with a good-looking broad."

"Did Steve say that?" she asked sharply.

"Say what?" His eyes were blue and innocent.

"Did he call me a broad?"

The eyes wavered. "Maybe he said lady, I'm not sure."

"Which was it?"

He was meek. "He said…a good-looking girl."

"Then why did you…Listen, Richard, where do you get these colorful phrases?"

"I read a lot," he said promptly.

"Somebody'd better censor your literary intake. Doesn't anybody *care?*"

He knew, at last, that he was being scolded. His face changed; he looked spanked. And of course she couldn't stand that chastened expression. "It's all right, I'm just slightly exhausted," she said hastily. "Pay no attention, I like you the way you are. And now it's your turn to mind the store, all right? I'm going to the *bano.*"

"Okay, Kelly," he said, cheered, and the shine came back to his face. He was humming when she left the table, snapping his fingers in time to the music that came from an inner room.

I'll be a *very* bad mother, she thought.

Before she left the powder room she ran a comb through her own hair and dabbed some scent behind her ears. So Steve Connaught had told Richard to spruce up a little. She gazed at herself in the glass and had a moment of depression. It was only a pick-up, after all. Tomorrow Steve would find another pretty face.

But it wasn't tomorrow yet. She went back to the table again.

Steve and Richard were talking; that was, Richard was talking and Steve was listening. She sat down. Richard was yakking away. "I don't like the present administration," he was saying passionately. "It's Fascist, now don't you agree with me? You'll see, too. People won't put up with it. Blood will run in the streets."

"You think so?" Steve asked with a grave face.

"I do! Times are changing. It's like the French Revolution. Have you read Rousseau?"

"I have a nodding acquaintance with him," Steve said without batting an eyelash.

"Well, he was the father of the French Revolution. He believed that man was good by nature but corrupted by civilization. And I believe that too, Steve."

"What do you think, Kelly?"

She looked across at Steve. "I think we'll have to table this discussion. Because, although it's been the greatest, I know someone who has to go beddy-bye."

"Not yet!"

"What Kelly says goes," Steve announced. "She's the one who's responsible for both of us. It's your bedtime and mine."

"Why do I have to be treated like a *child?*"

"For the next few years it's your fate," Steve said calmly, and snapped his fingers at the waiter across the room. Somehow, when he did it, it didn't irk Kelly. Obviously it didn't irritate the waiter either, because he hopped right over and scribbled out the chit.

Outside, in the cool and fragrant night air, they waited while Steve flagged down a cab. Richard sat in the middle, leaning just slightly toward Kelly. She had the feeling that, if she were to put an arm around him, he might lean all the way. But she couldn't bring herself to do it, though she wanted to. Somehow she liked his pride and admired his staunch independence. He might need love but, as with animals, one had to move slowly and cautiously. She didn't want to do anything that might damage that self-sufficiency. By all odds, it looked as if Richard might have need of that in the years to come.

CHAPTER 4

At almost midnight, the courtyard of the house on the Paseo de la Castellana was a melange of smells; jasmine, heady and sweet, and the woodsy redolence of the boungainvillea. Flowering shrubs gave off a cloying scent, the strongest of which was the gardenia, so potent that it was almost a sickish stench. A thin slice of moon, silver and dazzling, lit up the starry sky; stumbling over a hump of stone as they walked up to the house, under the trees and flowering bushes, Kelly caught at Steve's hand.

"All right?" he asked, grasping her.

"I'm fine. I think I drank too much."

"You had a few drinks, that's all. Don't be silly."

"That's Sirius," Richard said, looking upwards. "See? The bright star southward. What a night, boy."

The pretty little uniformed maid opened the door for them.

"*Buenas noches,*" she said, with her shy, dimpled smile. And then Joia joined them, coming down the stairs.

"I had such a good time," Richard told her excitedly. "We ate like pigs. Anyway, I did. As a matter of fact, we ate pig. With an apple in its nose. It was a super place, you could see right into the kitchens. Lots of blue tile."

"So then. All was good." The woman took Richard's hand. "I will put the boy to bed," she said softly. "The Senor will be with you shortly."

"But it's late. We won't bother him."

"He wishes to meet you. Please." She led the way into a different room from the one they'd been in earlier. It was a library, book-lined and spacious.

"Please sit down." The woman smiled her twisted smile and took Richard's hand again. "Say good-night, *querido.*"

"Good night. And thanks. It was great. I appreciate everything you've—"

"Okay, Rich," Steve said. "We all had a good time, didn't we?"

"Sure. It was…gee, swell."

"Now run up to bed."

"Yeah. Good night, Kelly."

"Good night, Richard."

"Jean Jacques Rousseau," Steve said, when they were alone. "The kid's got an I.Q. of probably 160. He could teach a class at Wesleyan. He's the original Quiz Kid."

"But he's such a *child*. Uptight, wouldn't you say?"

"Definitely."

Steve was roaming. "See this?" he said. "A Coromandel screen. Look at these Tang dynasty vases. There's a fortune in this room. I wonder—"

There was suddenly the sound of approaching footsteps. The man who came through the doorway, hand outstretched, was of medium height but with a large, senatorial head whose brow was massive, and the thick hair that sprang from it added to its impression of bigness. He was probably in his late fifties, and graying. His nose was aquiline and his lips thin, but his eyes were alert and soft in their expression. He was almost ugly, but his magnetism was immediately apparent. He was the kind of man of whom women would say, "He has something. I'm not sure what…but my God, it's *there*."

That, in fact, was Kelly's instant impression. That this man, in spite of his lack of beauty, was in some strange way enormously interesting…and attractive.

"So these are Richard's friends," he said. "This is *such* a pleasure. I just said good-night to the boy. Obviously he had a delightful time with you. I can't thank you enough for your thoughtfulness and generosity. I'm Richard's uncle, Constant Comstock." He was all charm. "You're Kelly? I've heard a great deal about you. And Steve? You must forgive me. Richard only mentioned first names."

He sat them down. "But it doesn't matter, does it? Why, that boy thinks the world of both of you." He pulled a cord and the little Spanish maid came into the room. "Maria, please. Something for us to drink."

The tiny little girl went out again, quietly.

"I understand you went to Botin's," Constant Comstock said. "Richard admitted that he wolfed down a huge dinner. How nice of you!"

"We enjoyed it," Steve said.

"But isn't he an interesting child? I think he's rather unusual. It means a great deal to me, you know, to have my nephew here. You see, I've no children of my own. My son was a victim of osteomyelitis. Donald died when he was only eight."

He smiled painfully. "There were no more. So I suppose you can understand how precious my brother's son is to me."

The little maidservant came in again, this time with a tray of liqueurs. "Oh, no," Kelly said, but her host insisted on pouring out some brandy for her. "You'll have scotch?" he said to Steve, who said that would be just fine. When the girl went out again there was a short but faintly uneasy silence. Kelly put an end to it. "You have a wonderful library," she said quickly.

"Yes. Do you like books?"

"Of course."

"So do I. They mean…oh, sometimes I think almost everything." His face came alive. "Words…they're deathless as long as libraries exist. Only the extinction of an entire civilization can blot them out forever."

He got up. "That's why I love this room," he said. "Well, for an example." He went over to the shelves and, at random, pulled out a slim volume.

Coming back to them, he held out the book, tapping his fingers on its cover.

"I made a haphazard choice," he said, smiling. "I see that I've picked a book of letters from sweethearts whose lives were far from tranquil." He held the book out. "Communications from Heloise to Abelard," he said. "Beautiful letters from agonized souls. Those two lustful, gifted human beings, whom life treated so shabbily. I adore them; I love the color of their time, all scarlet and gold. Their romance is one of the most potent love stories imaginable. Deeply physical, sensual and wildly abandoned, it was far from simply an engagement of the senses even from its beginning. Two marvellous minds came together by the merest accident and flamed into a passion that lit an imperishable blaze."

He sat down, holding the book in his hands as if he never wanted to let it go. "The letters of Heloise to Abelard," he said softly, "are a priceless legacy. The steadfast communion of these two fabled human beings from another time has stayed alive, an almost tangible thing, through the eight centuries that followed their span on earth."

He opened the book, leafed through it, and then closed it again. When he spoke once more his voice was even more hushed. "Separated in life by an obscene and senseless act of violence, this man and woman of the Moyen Age—no longer even dust— have remained joined in the annals of history and literature, their names forever united, a shining testimony to the transcendental power of love."

There was silence in the room. The light was fitful, coming from only one or two lamps. Shadows leaned across the carpet. There was no sound from beyond.

Then, astonishingly, Constant Comstock laughed. "I get carried away," he apologized. "You see, I'm a romantic, in love with history and the thrilling events of the past."

He laughed again. "You'll think me an eccentric. But I am!"

Steve said, "I wonder if that *extinction* of an entire civilization will come…one of these days."

"No."

"You don't think it will?"

"It won't." The voice was flat, authoritative. "I promise you that. Beauty and truth will be preserved. Forever. I know it."

"How can you be so sure?"

"Because I know. Because there are those of us who care so deeply about beauty, and the preservation of beauty, that they will do anything, *anything*, to check the advance of the barbarians."

"Well, good," Steve said, and Constant Comstock laughed again, looked delighted. "You're someone I like very much," he said, and apologized again. "Yes, I'm afraid I have a tendency to pontificate. Forgive me, this is not parlor talk. Tell me, have you been to Madrid before?"

"No."

"And you?" He looked at Kelly.

"I've been just about everywhere," she said. "I'm an airline employee. I've been working for ITA for four years and I know almost every corner of the globe."

"Wonderful." He turned to Steve again. "And you, sir?"

"The reason I bypassed Spain was political."

"But why now?"

"Because Spain was here long before Franco. As Germany and Austria were before the Anschluss. So you grow up a little."

"Yes, you do. I remember a time when I swore I'd never set foot on German soil. I got over it. One of the best fortnights I ever had was on a Rhine journey. And I never once thought of Hitler or the Storm Troopers."

"Sic transit," Steve murmured.

"Yes, sic transit. Well, I must say, I'm enjoying your company. And I hope, Mr. Connaught, that you will come to like this city. Of course it's not old. That is, in its present state. Like Lisbon, it's a modern metropolis. Why, today's Madrid is younger than St. Petersburg, Florida. It's younger than Boston."

"I didn't realize that," Kelly said.

"After all, this city was merely established as a bulkhead, in the form of a fortress to Toledo, and it wasn't until the sixteenth century that Philip the Second founded what was then a village as its capital. Compared to the eighth and ninth century cities, that's today's times."

He leaned forward to light a cigarette for Kelly, pushed an ashtray toward her. "And yet," he said, "there's something extraordinarily old-world about Madrid. To me, it's an exquisite city, with an ancient look. Go to the Plaza Mayor and you'll see a sign reading Canada. It means sheepwalk. Sheepwalks, here in Madrid and elsewhere, were established by royal decree centuries ago. And the law has never been countermanded. Sheep may legally be driven through the city, that is, if they keep to the official route."

It was obvious that Constant Comstock was playing to the galleries. Also that he was very aware of his young female guest; he was playing to her in particular. His eyes flattered her, told her she was a desirable creature. This was a man who liked women, as he liked admiration and respect. Yet he didn't sound unpleasantly pompous. He was learned, worldly and suave. Any woman of whatever age would respond to a man like this. No wonder he had shed a first wife for a second. Possibly there would be a third wife…and a fourth.

And then Steve got up, signaling Kelly with his eyes, after perhaps an hour's conversation. "We mustn't keep you any longer," he said. "I've enjoyed this, but it's getting late."

"I've enjoyed it too."

"Thanks for the drinks."

"My thanks to you. For taking my nephew out on the town."

"It was our pleasure."

"Perhaps. But I would like to reciprocate. I mean, for my own sake. I want you to meet my wife. Won't you take dinner with us tomorrow evening?"

The question was addressed mainly to Kelly.

"That's very nice, but—"

"That is, if it would be convenient for you."

She glanced up at Steve.

"It sounds fine," he said.

And so Steve accepted for both of them. "My wife will be very pleased," Comstock said. "Shall we make it at, let's say, eight o'clock?"

"Thank you."

"I'll be looking forward to it. I'm sorry you have to leave now. It really isn't very late, is it?"

"I've been doing some asking around," Steve said. "There's a place with flamenco dancing. In the old quarter. The Corral de la Moreria. I thought I'd like to take Miss Jones there to finish off the evening."

"A good place," their host said approvingly. "I think you'll like it. It's quite authentic."

He saw them to the door. "Have fun."

"Good night."

They went out again into the scented courtyard and a few steps away Steve latched on to a cab. He never asked Kelly if she was willing to go; he simply arranged everything and she went along with his plans.

He was that kind of man.

The Corral was a cellar dive, dark, candle-lit, with a faintly musty smell. They were given a table in the corner, where there was privacy, a little enclave of quiet in the noisy room. "How's this?" Steve asked.

"Wonderful."

"Would you rather have done something else?"

"No. This is nice, Steve."

"There's something fascinating about a country that comes alive only in the night hours," he said, and they watched the dancing. The flounced, tiered skirts of the woman flared and swirled. The male performer, lithe and slim-hipped, his high heels stamping, circled his partner in a primitive dance of lust.

It was wild, elemental, almost unbearably exciting. *"Ole,"* the spectators murmured at a particularly intricate turn or twist, and at the end, as the spotlights played dazzlingly over the dancers, they shouted, some getting to their feet. *"Brava…bravo…brava…"*

They left after an hour. In the taxi on the way back to the hotel, Steve said he was sorry if she was tired, but that he was too. "Yet there will never be a day much better than this one," he told her, and took her hand. He held it for a moment, then raised it to his lips. In a man like that, who looked so hard and self-sustaining, the unexpected gentleness of his mouth on the back of her hand was like a blessing. He could have grabbed her, kissed her, asked for something. But he didn't.

The elevator shuddered to a stop at her floor.

"Good night," Steve said. "Sleep well."

"You too."

She got out and the elevator door closed. She went to her room and the beat of the Catalan music was still in her heart and mind. I had a nice day, she thought and, exhausted, got into bed.

He could have done a selling job, she thought, and I might have given in. But he hadn't. She fell asleep thinking of his mouth, and the hard jut of his jaw.

A man named Steve…

CHAPTER 5

The sunlight pricked through the blinds. The telephone was ringing. I don't have to answer that, Kelly told herself, but she sprang out of bed.

It wasn't Steve. It was Richard.

"Did I call too early?" he asked.

"I don't even know what time it is."

"Oh, then I woke you up."

"It doesn't matter. I had to get up anyway, to answer the phone."

"Oh." Then he burst out laughing. "Ha ha," he said. "That's a good one." And he laughed some more.

"What is it you want, Richard?"

"Oh. It's just that…nobody said anything about today. Does that mean I'm on my own from now on?"

"What are you talking about?"

She was irritable. She had hoped to hear that dark voice, that hard, cool voice. I wanted it to be Steve, she thought.

"Oh, nothing," he said quickly. "It doesn't matter. I'm sorry if I'm getting in your hair, Kelly."

Instantly contrite, she apologized. "Honey, it's not that. I was up very late last night, that's all."

"Okay, good-bye."

"Just a minute, Richard." He sounded so woebegone, so abandoned. "Listen, do you want to do some sightseeing today? I'd be glad to take you."

"Super," he said, relieved, "Is Steve coming too?"

"Steve? I have no idea."

"Oh," he said, surprised. "I thought you were a couple."

She turned on her back and laughed. "Richard, I just—"

"In fact, I thought we were a trio. You know, like Athos, Porthos and—"

"We'll see. But for now, I'd like to get a little more shut-eye. I'll call you back in an hour. I promise."

"Groovy. I'll show you around this crazy house. It's spooky. I can find my way now, but at first—"

"Good-bye, Richard. In an hour," she said, and hung up the phone.

She was just drifting off to sleep again when the phone rang once more.

"Damn and double damn," she muttered, but raced for it just the same. This time it was Steve.

"Had breakfast?"

"No."

"Neither have I. Let's have it out on the terrace."

"All right."

"Tennish? Then we can go places and see things. The sheepwalks and all that."

"That sounds nice. Except that I'm obligated again."

"Richard?"

"Yes."

"I don't mind."

"I'm to call him back in an hour, and then I guess I'll have to make a stop off at his uncle's house."

"So what? See you at ten o'clock. Ask for Steve Connaught's table."

He rang off and she got into bed again. But only for a moment. Better get up, she thought. Look your best. You might never meet a man like that again.

•••

It was when she opened a drawer in the heavy Spanish chest that she knew someone had been in her room. Why? Because, used as she was to traveling light and neat, half in and half out of suitcases, she was meticulous about every item. And her lingerie was always arranged just so; for example, slips to the right, nightwear to the left, and in the center bras and pantyhose.

She stood and looked thoughtfully into the contents of the drawer. Everything was neat as a pin, except that there was a slip on the side with the nightgowns. Tidily folded, to be sure…but in the wrong place.

That wasn't her doing. Time being of the essence, she *never* made mistakes like that. There was no reason in the world for that slip to be where it was.

Once she got the idea in her mind, she went snooping. After a thorough search of the room she had to come to the conclusion that she was reaching at straws. Because there was nothing else out of place. It was only the nylon slip that was not where it should be.

It was the maid who did her room, she decided. The girl had been curious to see what the American Senorita's underwear was like. But it was almost with triumph that she discovered the other tell-tale sign. Just before she was ready to go downstairs, she realized that she would have to change pocketbooks to go with the dress she was wearing.

She opened her suitcase and got out the navy bag.

And as she started to transfer the contents of the one previously used, she saw a rip in the stitching of the navy handbag where the flap joined the body of the bag.

It was a sizeable tear. One which hadn't been there before; as a matter of fact, it was a recently-purchased bag.

Now she was certain. It hadn't been an inquisitive housemaid. It had been someone else, someone who had been in her room last night, when she was away. Someone had carefully gone through her things. But it was a very hasty search. Hence the two slipups… the slightly disarranged drawer in the chest and this damage to the handbag.

Her mind went back to the telephone call, the last one from Senor Nascimento. So that was it, she thought, He suspected her of swiping the pearls. And had decided to fine-toothcomb her room in an effort to retrieve them.

It had to be that.

How had he gotten into her room?

She carefully and methodically went over all her possessions again. There was nothing else awry. Of course it could have been the maid...

No, she thought. She was so used to travel. And particularly in Spain the hotel employees were painfully honest. It was such an impoverished country, yet the help everywhere was scrupulously trustworthy. Their pride was almost heartbreaking. In Italy, perhaps. But never, never Spain. And it was a truism that airline employees were handled with kid gloves everywhere.

However it had happened. Someone had been in this room last night.

She went outside to the terrace, looked up and down. It was the only terrace visible; she had never had this room before, but there was nothing above in the way of an outdoor accommodation. And it seemed almost impossible for anyone to gain access to this terrace from an adjoining building. The Gaudi house, with its grotesque, if interesting contours, was a good distance away, and the only possible means of climbing up would be from the windows below, which meant a particularly strenuous form of athletics. And anyway, how would it be easier for someone to get into the suite below?

Yet someone had been here, had canvassed the room and her belongings, and if it weren't for the rip in her handbag she would have been convinced that a wistful and curious little Spanish girl had glanced longingly at her finery in the drawer of the chest. There was nothing else amiss, and she was already late in meeting Steve. She locked her door and went down the corridor. There wouldn't be a second visit, she was sure. There was nothing hidden in her room and whoever had searched it must know that by now. But she cursed the day she had ever laid eyes on Senor and Senora Nascimento. She had enough troubles without theirs added to the rest of it.

•••

The outdoor terrace of the Hotel Fenix had several levels, each of them set on a plateau above stone steps. Cherry-red awnings shaded the round white tables. The foliage was lush and wonderful, the smells ineffable. Even the Ritz didn't have a garden like this.

Steve was sitting on the second level. He stood up when he saw her walking up the steps. There was an ice bucket with a bottle of Taittinger's nestled inside it.

"Champagne at ten in the morning?" she said.

"Yes, with fresh strawberries."

He filled a tulip glass for her. "To days of love and laughter," he said, clinking glasses. "You look rested. Of course it's because you're so young. These old red eyes of mine…"

She laughed. "You sound like Father Time."

"Sometimes I feel that way. Why are you looking so preoccupied?"

"Because something's on my mind." She sipped the champagne; the bubbles flew up her nose. The strawberries, in crystal bowls, smelled tangy and sweet.

"Tell me about it."

"Someone was in my room last night."

"What makes you think so?"

"I saw something wrong when I was getting dressed. Things were out of order in my lingerie drawer."

"Oh?"

"At first I blamed it on the girl who did my room. I just thought she wanted a peek at American silks and nylons. But later, when I got this handbag out of my suitcase, I had second thoughts. Look."

She showed him the tear.

"Sure you didn't do it yourself?"

"No, it's a brand new purse. Someone else did it, someone who was in a hurry to get out fast."

"How would that someone get in?"

"I don't know. Maybe found a way to get hold of a white coat so he'd look like a servant of the hotel. Somehow got the keys to my room."

"You say 'he.' "

"Well, I think it was Senor Nascimento."

"Looking for the missing pearls?"

"It's as good a guess as any."

"Maybe." But his smile was indulgent.

"Oh, I know they seemed substantial people. But there's something going on, and when I spoke to Senor Nascimento and said Richard wanted to see them again, he shrugged it off. They *are* questionable, Steve. I sense it. And they didn't want me to show up at their house. He called for the bag at the hotel here."

"Okay, if you feel that way, let's follow it up."

"How?"

"Go and see them, whether they like it or not."

"I guess it's better to just forget about it."

"If I thought someone entered my room without my knowledge, I wouldn't want to forget about it."

"Well, I don't know. We'll see."

"Meanwhile, let's finish this bottle."

"Fine, but can we order soon?"

"Party pooper." But he called over the waiter.

They ate a hearty breakfast, had coffee and a last cigarette and then Kelly said that Richard must be waiting impatiently for her call. "All right, you ring him and I'll snag a cab," Steve said, and they went down the steps into the lobby again.

Richard cut in on the conversation between Kelly and one of the servants. "Hey, is that you?" he asked.

"Richard?"

"Hi. Are you coming around soon?"

"We're just leaving the hotel. Steve's outside, getting a taxi."

"I'm ready," he said. "I'll open the door for you. It's a nice day, isn't it?"

"Yes, lovely."

"I'm all ready," he said again, and she hung up the phone, picturing him looking earnestly out the paned glass of the entrance door, waiting for his friends.

And it *was* Richard who swung open the door for them. *"Buenas dias,"* he said, his face flushed with eagerness. "Say, this is great. Hello, Steve. Come on in."

Joia came down the stairs and said good morning to them.

"I wanna show them my room," Richard said.

"But, Richard—"

"It's all right," Joia murmured. "The Senora is sleeping."

"C'mon up. This is really a very nice house."

They followed him up the stairs. And yes, it was a beautiful house, built around a central, interior courtyard. Long, windowed balconies stretched out on corridors with rooms to the right. Richard's bedroom looked out onto the back, with a view of sweeping trees and blooming bushes. The louvres were slatted against the sun.

"Do you like it?" the boy asked them.

"Richard, it's lovely."

"A nice place to visit," he said. "But I wouldn't want to live here."

"Well, you're only stopping off here, isn't that so?"

"I don't know. I think my uncle wants me to stay. He's making everything highly attractive. He claims he's very fond of me."

"Well, I suppose he is. That's only natural, isn't it? What's this, Richard?"

He dashed over. "My diary." His hand closed over it. "It's rather private, you know."

"Oh, I see."

"Some day I'll write my memoirs."

Kelly's eyes met Steve's, and it was in that moment that she was lost. His strong, carved face was tender, so understanding…

A man who liked kids.

That's all I needed, she thought, turning away quickly.

Every big city in the world had its Flea Market. In Madrid it was the Rastro; every kind of article could be bought there. It was divided into two parts, the antiques and the second-hand goods. The sophisticated buyer could always hope to unearth a painting that might net him a small fortune or a first edition or anything that might have escaped the vendors' expertise.

Richard bought a silver crucifix for Joia.

It was wrapped for him and he pulled a wallet out of his pocket, stuffed with paper money. "Richard," Kelly said, dazed. "Where did you get all that cash?"

"Pushing drugs," he said tersely.

"Is that supposed to be funny?"

"It was supposed to be," he said. "But apparently it landed with a dull thud."

Steve turned away, hiding a smile.

"What can I buy you?" Richard asked. "I want to buy you something nice, Kelly."

"I don't want anything. Put that money away."

"I *will* buy you something," he insisted. "If you won't tell me I'll just have to guess."

"Darling, nothing."

"Then you'll just have to accept my choice."

He made her stay where she was, and then went browsing. He came back a short while later with a large box. He held it out to her. "I hope you like this," he said.

"Oh, Richard."

"Let's get something for Steve."

He selected, for Steve, a beautiful glass paperweight. "Now I have to get something for my uncle," he said.

"Do you mind?" Kelly asked Steve, as they followed Richard around.

"No, let the kid have his fun. I'm rather enjoying it." He took her hand. "How about you?"

"Yes. Very much."

Richard found an old edition of an eighteenth century book on medieval music. "He can add it to his library, you know."

"Richard, this costs 2500 pesetas. That's a great deal of money."

"It doesn't matter. I have lots of money. Oh, yeah, one thing more," he said. "Something for my aunt."

"Dolores?"

"No, Aunt Elizabeth. I'll have it sent."

And he did. He bought a jade bracelet, which came to 5500 pesetas, and when he put his wallet in his pocket again it was still crammed with notes. But it was touching; quite clearly Uncle Constant's first wife held a very special place in this little boy's heart. "She'll like it," he said. "I *hope*."

"Now how about lunch?" Steve asked.

"But Richard didn't get anything for Dolores."

"Do I have to?"

"I'm afraid so. You got something for your uncle."

"Okay. Let's see…"

He started browsing again.

"That," he said finally, pointing.

It was a golden canary in a gilded cage. The sweet voice of the bird trilled, as the tiny throat quivered with ecstasy.

"Richard, she wouldn't want that."

"Why not? She's a bird herself, in a gilded cage."

His face was calm and serious. Kelly turned him away from the little canary and directed him to a stall with Florentine trinketry. "Get her some earrings," she said, and at her bidding, he bought some filigreed drops for pierced ears.

"Now can we have luch?" Steve asked patiently.

"I thought you wanted to go to the Stamp Market."

"Richard would only buy stamps for all his friends and relatives. I'm hungry."

"Me too," Richard said.

They ate at an outdoor cafe near the Plaza Mayor, after going down a flight of ancient steps into the beautiful square; their table faced the plaza, an architectural splendor almost as gorgeous as the Place de Vosges in Paris. The gazpacho was cool and refreshing, the cold beef like butter. And then they got into a taxicab which took them to the Toledo Bridge, where they got out and walked. Later, they found a fascinating winding street of houses, got out and walked again, and after that viewed the city from the Casa de Campo, with its soaring, twisted cypresses sketched across an almost cloudless sky.

At five o'clock they took Richard home. He had been gratified to hear that they were dining with his family. "And you must open your present as soon as you're home," he told Kelly.

When she had left Steve, agreeing to meet him in the lobby at seven-thirty, she unwrapped Richard's gift before lying down to nap.

It was a pearline shell, a chambered nautilus, the hollows of which wound round and round, with a secret heart at the innermost cavern at the core of the nacreous husk. If you put it to your ear you could hear the sea sounds, the primeval roar of the waters of the earth, the mysterious signallings of the beginnings of man.

She held the beautiful object in her hands. She was almost crying inside. That stuffed wallet…the pesetas Richard had dribbled away in the course of the morning. This lovely thing had been, of all of them, the least expensive, costing practically nothing. Yet it was the loveliest present he had bought. His values were perfect. Money didn't have any meaning for him, but beauty did, and he had made her the finest present of all.

There could be nothing more exquisite than this treasure from the sea, washed up onto the sands.

She got into bed and closed her eyes. The chambered nautilus was clasped to her. And with the silky, cool shell against her breast, she slept.

It was nice to know that a little boy knew how to please, that he hadn't given her a bracelet, or a silver trinket, but something from the earth and the natural elements. And that he instinctively knew what it would mean to her. It was a wonderful thing…and that a child could know so much.

CHAPTER 6

"What do you want?" the man who opened the door-asked.

"I have something for you."

"For me? What is it?"

"Something you have been missing."

"What do you mean?"

"May I come in?"

There was no question about the stranger's coming in. His foot was firmly wedged in the door. The little man with the croupy voice said, "I'll call the—"

"The police? I don't think so. You don't want to talk to the police, do you?"

There was a silence. And then, "I understand you have been looking for these," the man at the door said, taking a double strand of pearls out of his pocket. The pearls were nestled inside a white linen handkerchief with the embroidered initials J.N.

"Now may I come in, Jorge Nascimento?"

The visitor was there for over an hour. During that time the Senor was more than uncomfortable; he was profoundly distressed. It was pointed out to him, for example, that the man who sat across from him knew about the narcotics transactions, knew about the pipeline from Turkey, was well acquainted with the vice connections in Tunis.

"Nothing can be proved," the Senor said languidly.

"Possibly. But there is still the dossier on you."

"There is a dossier on millions of persons."

"Very true."

"Nothing can be proved. You must know that."

"But this can be proved," the other man said, dangling the pearls in front of him. "I made several transatlantic telephone calls. Tiffany's, Van Cleef and Arpels. And Carrier's." He smiled. "I understand that a double strand of Oriental pearls was cleverly spirited out of one of those stores a week ago."

Then he shook his head admiringly. "How did you manage it?"

"I don't know what you are talking about."

"They would recognize you, isn't that so?"

After a while the Senor said, "What do you want? How much?"

"Not money."

"Then what?"

It was explained what. And further explained what it would mean to Senor Nascimento in terms of good, hard cash. The terms were very good.

There was a long pause. "It's not in my line," the Senor said, regretfully. "You want the Spanish Mafia."

"I want you. And I have you. Why should I look further?"

He rolled the pearls up in the handkerchief. "I assume we have reached an agreement."

"I will have to think it over."

"No, you won't, my friend." The visitor's face was quiet, grave, cold. "It means danger for me too, but it's the only way, and the stakes are high."

"Who are you?"

"It doesn't matter who I am. I have access to diplomatic channels, let's put it that way. Many people would be surprised at what I know. People who think themselves totally in the clear. But then, this doesn't concern us now. You're not a stupid man. You've covered your tracks neatly enough. You're right when you say nothing can be proved. *Yet.* Except for this. That was a bad mistake on your part. Aren't you rich enough?"

He patted his pocket. "The underwriters would be delighted to find the person who stole these. I was informed that the last persons to look at gems, just before the theft of this little haul was discovered, was a Spanish-speaking couple. The woman felt ill, asked for a glass of water, and then, in a most dramatic way, fainted."

His smile was again admiring. "I didn't think such a simple trick would work any more. But obviously, it did."

After a thoughtful silence Senor Nascimento said, "When?"

"There will be further instructions."

"What about those?" Senor Nascimento asked, pointing to the other man's pocket.

"They're yours. When the job is done."

"How can I be sure of that?"

The visitor laughed. He patted his pocket. "This is chicken feed compared to—"

He broke off. "You'll get them back," he said.

•••

The Comstock villa, at eight o'clock, was jewel-lit; from the vantage point of the front courtyard it looked like fairyland, with every window, it seemed, blazing golden. The two visitors were shown into still another *sala*, this one obviously a main salon, a very large room comfortably furnished and quite clearly the family room of the household.

Constant Comstock joined them almost immediately, holding out a welcoming hand to each. Drinks were brought in, scotch for Steve, dry gin for Kelly, and when Richard came down a few minutes later, a coke for him, tinkling with ice in a glass. "I understand you went to the Rastro," their host said, and there was general conversation about the Madrid Flea Market.

"Richard gave me a wonderful music book, you know."

"He gave me a beautiful shell," Kelly said.

"Did you like it?"

"I adore it. I'll always keep it."

"Good, I'm glad. I—"

"Buenas noches" a voice said suddenly, and a breathtakingly beautiful woman stood in the archway between the rooms.

Kelly stared, conscious of Steve's sharpening eyes, and felt a small pang as she watched his face and thought, if I were a man I'd gasp too.

Constant got up and so did Steve. The young woman came forward. She had olive-tinted skin, pale blonde hair piled into a chignon on top of her head, amber eyes and long, slender legs. Her hands, as she extended them, were slim and with long-tipped nails.

As her husband made the introductions Kelly caught sight of the expression on his face, which was one of deep pride and infatuation. And when everyone was seated, he watched her intently as she manufactured some small talk. His eyes were on her every minute. She chattered, not mindlessly, but without brilliance of phrase, yet eyeing her husband, Kelly realized that Constant Comstock prized this particular acquisition of his very highly.

He was a born collector, with a taste for amassing beautiful objects, and this gorgeous young woman was a cherished possession, it was clear. And yet there was something about Dolores that smacked of the streets, a certain manner of speech which suggested that she came from a lower stratum of society from her husband. Kelly decided that Dolores was not high-born, but had come from pedestrian surroundings; however she had learned how to play the social game and did it very well.

That was, until her third cocktail. After that she effervesced a bit too much, laughed a little too loudly, and her lovely eyes were slightly filmed. At that point her husband took over and directed the conversation.

It was really very pleasant. A beautiful house, a beautiful room, delightful flower smells and excellent talk—for Constant Comstock was an erudite man and a gifted anecdotist. He was plainly taken by Steve, and was giving him a rough itinerary of some of the things to see in Madrid.

"The Cathedral of La Almudena. It's to the left of the Palace and has a facade in the neo-classical manner. Also the Church of San Francisco el Grande, the interior of which has a great dome which was decorated by Goya."

"Steve's a Goya buff," Kelly said.

"I don't blame him. So am I."

"Oh, but those awful war pictures," Dolores said, shuddering.

"That's only one phase of his work," her husband said, looking indulgent. "Well, for me, of course, the second hand bookstalls on the Cuesta de Moyano are a great lure. I have found many of my treasures there. If you have any bibliophilic leanings, that's the place to go."

"I'll keep it in mind."

"And don't bother going to the Flea Market again. Go to the Calle de Cervantes. In a small quarter there I stumbled across a sale of paintings and sculptures. It didn't look like much, but behind a jumble of junk I found one of those attenuated bronze figures. Of course it couldn't be a Giacometti. Everyone is imitating Giacometti. However, I decided to buy it anyway; obviously the dealer thought it a fake but had priced it fairly high, reasoning that some fool would take it for the real thing and gamble on it. What do you think?"

"It was the real thing," Steve hazarded, rolling his cigar to the other side of his mouth.

"It was, it was!"

"Oh, could I see it?" Steve asked, leaning forward.

There was a sudden, rather loud laugh from Dolores. It was almost a hoot. Her husband looked quickly at her and then said, "Am I boring you, darling?"

He didn't wait for an answer. "Of course I am," he said to the others. "She wants to talk about herself. All women want to do that. You see, she was a model when I met her. A very bad one, but that was the only thing she knew how to do."

"Don't listen to this man. I was a very good model. Of course I was looking all the while for someone to take care of me."

"So you admit it," Comstock said.

"Certainly, *si*. Otherwise, why are we women? If you are beautiful you deserve the best."

It was said without the slightest trace of self-consciousness. Or even with vanity. It was simply stated as a fact.

"However," she went on, "I picked the wrong man. I thought he was rich."

It was taken as a joke until Kelly saw the faint flush on the man's cheekbones. At the same time Dolores sent a challenging, defiant look her husband's way. There was a small, rather uncomfortable silence and then Constant said, "All women want to be Jacqueline Onassis. With unlimited funds."

"All women want security," she cried, and this time her expression was decidedly unpleasant. "All right, show them the Giacometti," she said. "Go on, our guests want to see it."

The flush had risen on Comstock's face. "Dolores…*if* you please," he said quietly.

"You know why you won't see it?" the woman said. "Because he sold it. To a gallery in New York. It brought in a lot of money. So you see, until the last piece is sold, we live very comfortably."

She settled back in her chair, looking satisfied, as if she had gratified her desire to wound her husband. And she had certainly succeeded. By this time Constant Comstock was almost livid.

Steve broke the ugly silence. "It costs a bundle to live these days. Who doesn't feel the pinch?"

Just the same, their host had lost some of his aplomb, That he was upset and angry, and embarrassed as well, was evident. "We still have a few minutes before the meal will be served," he said, getting up. "I thought you might like to see the gardens."

They went through to the back of the house. There were delightful little salons on either side of a long, columned passageway and then there was a kind of enclosed atrium, with open windows on either side. The gardens sprang into view through the apertures and then they were outside, in a veritable paradise. Poplars and twisted cypresses and plane trees stood high, and the flowering bushes, crimson and pearly white and deep pink, with the glory of the ubiquitous purple, like the mantle of a Herod, abounded. It was cool now, with a soft, whispering breeze.

"What a way to live," Steve muttered to Kelly, as they walked the tiled paths.

"I could get used to it in no time," she murmured back.

At the end of the driveway, to the far left of the gardens, was a large garage, vine-covered. The doors were open and there was a glimpse of two cars inside. One was the limousine that had been standing outside the previous evening. And as they stood there, with Comstock explaining that this beautiful bush was a Glorioso and in spite of its marvelous beauty was almost a weed, the chauffeur came out of the garage and closed the doors.

Kelly's mind flashed back to the snapshot which had been taken at Botin's. Yes, it was the same man. Now she was certain. He stood while the doors telescoped together, turned, raised a finger in the direction of his employer and employer's wife, and then strode past them, on the balls of his feet, disappearing round a bend in the path.

But not before Kelly saw the narrowed eyes of her host. He was looking closely at his wife, whose perfect, chiseled face was calm and indifferent. The picture shifted into a more distinct focus. Why, he's jealous, she thought. Watchful, suspecting...

Her eyes met Steve's, and she saw that he was thinking the same thing. Shades of *Lady Chatterly's Lover*, Kelly mused, and turned discreetly away. A few minutes later she asked Richard if he would direct her to the bathroom and when they were inside the house he took her upstairs.

"Can you find your way back down?" he asked. "Or shall I wait?"

"I can find my way."

"Holler if you need me."

"Don't worry."

She came out a few minutes later, took a wrong turning and, blundering into the adjunct to a suite of rooms, heard raised voices, was about to turn away when, reflected in a large pier glass inside the rooms off the hall, she saw the figures of her host and hostess.

They were glaring at each other.

"You're a vulgar bitch," Constant was saying.

"You're a pauper!"

"You stupid slut. You never had it so good. I took you out of the gutter."

"Stop screaming at me. They'll hear downstairs."

"I don't care if all Madrid hears."

"How amusing! You, of all people! Your respectability means more to you than—"

"What respectability? I gave up a good woman and married a—"

"Don't say it," Dolores ground out. "If you say it I'll kill you. I mean it. I'll…"

"Shut your mouth," he flashed back, in a strangled voice. "All you really want is bed, you bird-brained bitch. Don't think I don't know what's going on. That truckdriver, that animal…"

He put a hand in her hair and dragged her head backwards. "Just let me catch you. Then we'll see who kills whom."

A cry of pain was wrested from the woman's lips. Wide-eyed, wanting only to get back downstairs, Kelly was nevertheless transfixed by the drama inside. And then, as another cry burst from Dolores, the man's arms went around her. There was a protesting struggle.

"*I hate you…*"

"You don't hate me," he said.

"I do!"

"You don't. But I wouldn't care if you did. You'll stick with me and you know it. Who else would put up with you? There are a million women better looking than you and I could have any one of them. I could have a woman with money. Don't you think so? Instead of pouring out thousands of pesetas practically by the hour on a gutter woman. I taught you how to behave and how to dress and—"

There was a glimpse of the woman's eyes in the glass. They were suddenly terrified. She was really afraid of losing Constant, Kelly thought. She was afraid to move for fear of being discovered a party to this lurid scene. If they should see her there…

And then Dolores sagged. She stopped struggling and ground passionately up against her husband. The fight had left her. She was totally submissive now.

The sound of Constant Comstock's hard breathing was upsetting…and disgusting, somehow. As quietly as she could manage, Kelly tiptoed down the carpeted corridor and found the stairs.

So that's what it was. Love and hate and rivalry. God knew what went on in this bizarre household.

Turn over a rock and all sorts of things crawled out.

"Well, you were gone long enough," Steve said. "What did you do, take a bath?"

He must have seen her discomfiture and her attempt to hide it. He lit her cigarette and, in her ear, asked what was wrong. She shook her head in the direction of Richard, and he got the message.

After a quarter of an hour or so Constant came in, apologizing for leaving them. "So sorry," he said. "I had a business call."

He picked up Steve's empty glass and refilled it, then insisted on pouring a little more into Kelly's still half-filled glass, and opened another coke for Richard. "Where's Dolores?" the boy asked. "Aren't we going to eat soon?"

"Dolores has a slight headache," his uncle said, and turned to the others. "Men get ulcers, women headaches." His smile was the usual charming one. "I'm sure she'll join us in a second or two and yes, Richard, we are going to have dinner soon."

Shortly afterwards Dolores came, tidied up, and they went into the dining room. The meal was excellent, beautifully served. Kelly was urged to tell about her adventures in flight; she related an anecdote or two.

"You must meet many interesting people," Dolores said.

Yes, she did, Kelly agreed. "For example, I met a very interesting young man on my last flight."

"Really?" Dolores leaned forward breathlessly.

"Richard."

There was laughter.

Richard laughed too, rather sheepishly. "I imagine I was kind of a pain in the neck for a while. But Kelly put up with me. And of course the Senor and Senora kind of took me off her hands."

"About whom are you talking?" Constant asked.

Steve said, "A very nice Spanish couple who took Richie under their wing."

"I sat very still," Richard said. "So that the Senora could wind the wool around my hands. She was knitting."

Long afterwards, Kelly remembered that it was Steve who said, "And then he broke her pearls."

"How come?" Constant asked, looking at his nephew.

"I never did know," Richard said, "but they broke, and then everyone was looking under their seats. It was okay, they were all found. And she was very nice about it."

"It turned out to be a cause celebre," Steve said.

"How was that?" Constant asked interestedly, and Steve looked at Kelly. "Ask her," he said. "She was the one who had to straighten things out."

"What happened?" Comstock asked.

"Oh, they called me," she said. "The husband phoned my hotel, very distressed. What happened was that when the pearls broke the Senora stuffed them in the bottom of her knitting bag and asked Richard to carry it for her. Then apparently they were held up at Customs and your driver spirited Richard away, still with the knitting bag."

"You don't say!"

"I'm sure they didn't expect anything like that. I have a feeling they were bringing in expensive goods and that they exploited Richard to get past Customs."

"Richard, you didn't tell me any of this!"

"I didn't think it was pertinent, Uncle Constant."

"How is it you didn't give back the bag?"

"It was Jose. I told him, but he only laughed at me and made me get in the car." Richard took a last bite of his *entrecote* and then neatly laid his knife and fork across the plate. "But anyway, I fixed it up. When I got here I was put to bed and then I called the hotels and found out where Kelly was staying. Then I went around there and gave her the bag."

His uncle looked stunned. "The devil you did!"

"I had to," Richard insisted.

"It's really all right," Kelly said. "I had a taxi take him home here again."

"But this is fascinating," Dolores said. "Tell me, Senorita, have you been, at some time, in a plane that was…how you call it?" She smiled helplessly and lifted her shoulders. "*You* know…where it should go to a place and then someone makes it go somewhere else?"

"Hi-jacked?" Steve suggested.

"Yes, yes."

"Not yet," Kelly said.

"It happens often, *si?* To Cuba?"

"Do you mind?" their host said peremptorily. "I'm concerned with Richard's foray into unfamiliar territory." He eyed his nephew. "So you left your bed and went traipsing around through the city," he said testily. "I don't know what to think about that, Richard."

"I had to get the bag back," Richard said stubbornly.

"He's here safe, can't you see?" Dolores said, gesturing. "So in the end everything came out all right."

"Not quite," Steve said, and Kelly was quite displeased with him. It would have been better to leave it where it had ended.

"What do you mean by that?" Comstock asked.

"Ask Kelly," Steve said.

Comstock shifted his attention. "What does he mean?"

"Oh, just that I had another call. Senor Nascimento thanked me for the return of the bag, but he claimed that the pearls weren't in it."

"And?" Dolores asked, her eyes bright and curious.

"I said I was sorry, but that I didn't know anything about it. I never looked inside the bag. There were more pressing matters."

"She had a date with me," Steve said.

Dolores clapped her hands. "Adventure!" she cried. "What fun you have, Senorita Kelly. My life is so dull. I should do something like that. Yes, Constant?"

"Um hum. We must talk about it some more. But right now I know someone whose bedtime it is."

"Not yet," Richard pleaded.

"It's way past time." Constant tinkled a little bell and the pretty little girl came in. "Joia, please," he said, and a few minutes later the deformed woman came into the room.

"Say good-night," Richard's uncle said.

The boy stood up reluctantly.

"Good night, everyone."

"Kiss your aunt."

Richard went dutifully over and put his mouth against Dolores' cheek. Then he shook his uncle's hand and, passing Kelly and Steve, said gruffly, "Thanks for everything."

"See you subsequently, all right?" Steve said.

"I hope so."

And then Joia took him up to bed.

• • •

It was later, in the library, that a few things became clear. Steve and Dolores were deep in a conversation of their own; Kelly thought, she's a born man-eater. Please, God, don't let her swallow Steve whole.

"I want to show you a rare edition of GIL BLAS," Constant said, guiding her into the book-lined library. "Elzevier…I picked them up in Paris. That is, three of the volumes. I had to hunt six years for the fourth."

He pulled out four tiny, leather-bound books, scarcely larger than the miniature address book she carried in her purse. "I found the final volume in Vienna," he said. "Of course I advertised, and at last my efforts bore fruit." He laughed. "I paid three times as much for the fourth book as I paid for the other three combined. Five thousand schillings. The law of supply and demand, of course. But it gave me this complete set, and some day it will be worth its weight in gold." He stroked the tiny books. "Aren't they pretty," he murmured, as if he were talking about a woman.

"Very pretty."

"I love *things*," he said. "Beautiful things. It's a curse, possibly. I can't help myself."

There was a brief silence and then he put the books aside. "Well," he said, "you've been very good to my nephew. You and your friend."

"It was easy. He's a nice child. We both like him a great deal."

"So do I. He's a very lost little boy."

"Do you think so?"

"I know so. And I'm not at all happy about his future."

She didn't know what to say, so she murmured, "I understand your brother is in Afghanistan."

"In…" He stared at her. "My brother?"

She looked up quickly. "Oh, did I misunderstand? I naturally assumed that you were Richard's father's brother."

"I am."

"Then—"

"But my brother, Richard's father, died over a year ago."

It was like a punch in the stomach. *Richard's father died a year ago?* Mr. Comstock saw her consternation and sat her down. "Tell me," he said, kind and steady and reassuring. "Just tell me what this is all about."

She told him. "Richard said his father was off somewhere…in Afghanistan and that he was a financier."

"He *was* a financier," Comstock said. "When he was alive. But he died about fourteen months ago, of a coronary. Lawrence was four years older than I, and I'm fifty-nine. His wife—"

His face hardened. "His wife is barely thirty. And a reprehensible, worthless person."

He recovered himself at once. "Never mind. About my brother…he was a brilliant man. He was early on involved with the idea of a European Common Market. Of course he worked too hard. I daresay he was a rotten husband; that's the only apologia I can make for Lisa, Richard's mother. At any rate, last April Larry suffered a coronary, a serious infarction. He died early in the morning, on the sixteenth. I got the call—"

He fell silent.

Kelly, stunned, tried to absorb this incredible bit of information. Did Richard believe his father was still alive? Or did he only want to pretend, to others, that he wasn't an orphan? Was it pride or fantasy?

"Is his mother Italian?" she asked. "Richard said something about a cousin, Gisela."

"Oh, that," Comstock said impatiently. "One of those ridiculous things. Yes, Lisa is Roman-born. And I believe there's some nonsense about an arranged marriage. If he talked about that, it's more or less true. But still a lot of hogwash. These paternalistic Italian families. I have no patience with it."

He tapped his fingers on the arm of his chair. "You really mean to say that Richard told you his father was—"

"He said his father was in Afghanistan. His mother, he told me, was in Rome. Although he didn't seem to be quite sure."

"*I'm* sure," Constant said. "She *is* in Rome. Which is why I sent for my nephew. You see…"

He hesitated, looked tentatively at her and then, apparently making up his mind, rose. "Do you mind waiting for a few minutes?" he asked. "There's something I'd like you to see."

"Yes, all right."

He was back shortly, with a newspaper clipping.

It was from a Rome newspaper, an item circled in red ink. "You don't speak or read Italian, by any chance?" he asked.

"I'm afraid not."

"Then let me read this release to you."

She sat back and listened. "It's a rather free translation," he admitted. "But you'll get the gist." He cleared his throat and then read aloud.

An American woman, Mrs. Lawrence Comstock of New York City, was asked to leave the Hotel Excelsior this A.M. when two men fought with knives in the suite occupied by Mrs. Comstock. One man was severely injured and hospitalized at the Ospadele Miseracordia. The American Consulate drew a curtain over the incident, and Mrs. Comstock apparently took up residence in other quarters.

He stopped reading, and looked up. "There's more," he said. "But that's the meat of it. Not a very pretty picture, is it?"

"No." She was sickened. Oh, poor little Richard.

"Lisa, my sister-in-law, is still a stunning woman," Comstock said. "When I first saw her, I almost fell in love with her myself. But if she keeps on the way she's going, she will be a wreck by the time she's forty."

His face took on an almost fanatical look. "I don't really like women," he admitted. "Most of them are vile…and disgracefully selfish…uncaring…"

There was a long, uncomfortable silence, and then he laughed rather sheepishly, his face clearing again. "That's an outrageous thing to say to someone who's a captive audience," he apologized. "Please forgive me. Perhaps I've known the wrong women in my life. At any rate, I ask your pardon. But to get to the heart of the matter. This article…" he crackled the newspaper clipping, "was instrumental in my arranging for Richard to spend some time here with us. My wife is not the most domestic woman in the world, but she has a certain earthy stability. We live a fairly normal life here at the Casa Bondadosa, and I—"

He looked at her. "What would you do?" he asked. "Wouldn't you want to intervene?"

"I don't know. I do think it's…sad."

"It's disgraceful." His face grew hard and stern again. "I can't allow it. Lawrence wouldn't have wanted me to countenance it. These are Richard's formative years, and I owe my brother something. I can't simply close my eyes and let that…that dissolute, irresponsible woman wreck the boy's life."

He folded up the clipping and put it down on a table top. "I don't know what's going to become of the child, but I've decided to take some kind of stand." He gave her a long look. "But this is family business, and I shouldn't bother you with it. It's just that you've been so good to my nephew, and I know that you have some inkling of his needs and lacks…and problems. But let's get off the subject of that child. Are you going back home right away?"

"No, as a matter of fact I've arranged it so that I'm taking some time off. My plans are to fly to Malaga and then rent a car. Drive through the Andalusian countryside, ending at Seville, where I'll hop to Lisbon and resume work on a 747."

"That sounds fine. I was seventeen when I first saw Andalusia. Just before starting college. I'll never forget its fascination. Do you know Da Falla? 'Nights in the Gardens of Spain?' That composer caught the cadence of it, the perfumed beauty and the ancient decadence. Oh yes, I envy you your first Andalusian trip. It will bring you joy."

"I hope so."

"Oh, but I'm sure it will."

• • •

"It's only a little after one," Steve said, as they climbed in a taxicab when they left the Villa Bondadosa, "I thought we could spend an hour or two in the Perico Chicote's Museum of Drinks, at one or another of the places."

"Who told you about that?"

"Miguel, at the desk. How about it?"

"I don't mind. I'll sleep late in the morning."

They went to the San Jeronimo, a tiny little bar just off the Espoz y Mina, where mink-caped ladies, seated at miniscule round tables, mingled with local butchers and taxi drivers. The air was thick with tobacco fumes and the reek of candles on the table tops. They drank sangria, sucking the fruit at the bottom of the pitcher, and laughed quite a bit.

"Oh, before I forget," Steve said after a while. "What was that business when you came downstairs from the little girls' room? You looked a little flushed. What's the story?"

She told him about it.

"It wasn't that I *wanted* to watch," she said. "I was just so afraid I'd be spotted. And then they got very occupied with each other. At that point they were oblivious to everything else."

"Sounds like a foreign film," he said. "So she was a prostitute when he met her."

"She was a model."

"It says here in fine print."

"I suppose she was a prostitute. That was made rather clear."

"She's a gorgeous gal."

"Yes."

"Empty, though."

"Well—"

"Come on, she's meat, that's all."

"Steve, that's a harsh judgment."

He looked uncontrite. "There are two kinds of women," he said. "Good ones and bad ones."

"I think that's simplistic." She was a little bit angry.

"No, it's not."

"It's a man's point of view."

"What are you, Fem Lib?"

"Not at all! I just don't agree with you."

"I didn't ask you to."

"Okay, then, okay."

"We're having a little fight," he said delightedly. "I like that. Our first quarrel. Shall we kiss and make up?"

"Go to hell."

"Listen," he said. "I *know*. I was married once. And burned. So I know whereof I speak."

"You were married?"

"For two years. It was a mistake. A fantastic mistake."

"What happened?"

"What do you think happened? She wasn't exactly true blue, but I had to find out the hard way." His face was bitter.

"I'm sorry."

"Happens all the time," he said, and lit a cigar. "Why not to me?"

There was nothing else for a while. Then Steve leaned back. "Look, I'm not crying in my beer. I'm not a cripple. I have all my arms and legs. 'Life is unfair,' Jack Kennedy said, and it's so. I just happened to meet you, and it looks good. The way you treat Richard. You're one of the good ones. That means everything to me. All right, I was nasty about Scarsdale. But you have good, honest values. I admit I wouldn't care about that if you were plain, or if you were cross-eyed. That's the way we are. Men, and women too. We like pretty things, shiny things. It's not equitable, but unfortunately nobody wants unpleasantness. Kelly, you're a darling girl. There was someone on the flight with the most wonderful face—"

"You mean Wendy Warren."

"I don't know what her name was, but she was a looker. But I didn't want her. She left me cold. I saw you, and that was that."

"Steve, you said you were burned. It can happen again."

"No," he said. "Because it was partly my fault. I didn't really love her. I was too young."

He put his cigar, smoldering, in an ashtray, "I'm not young any more," he said tiredly, passing a hand through his hair. "I won't make the same mistakes I made before."

He exhaled a stream of smoke. "And now you know. I wanted to tell you that. It was a bad time in my life. I guess I thought you should see me in another light. Someone who's been hurt. And anyway, the truth. So you won't think I'm just playing around."

She started to say something and he held up a hand. "There were no kids," he said. "No complications. I consider that important. I'm my own man. I never married again. She did."

A guitarist stopped at their table, waiting to hear their request number. "Kelly?" Steve asked.

" 'Tierra del Ensueno'," she suggested, off the top of her head, and the man strummed his instrument and sang the lovely song, his voice tender and caressing.

Steve gave him a hundred peseta bill when he had finished, and the man glowed at the size of the tip, wanting to know what else the Senor and Senora wished to hear.

"It's enough," Steve said brusquely. "Thank you very much, *amigo*."

• • •

At three in the morning Steve held up a finger outside on the Espoz y Mina. A car pulled up and they piled in. "Hotel Fenix," Steve said, and held Kelly's hand. "It was nice?" he asked.

"Lovely."

About five minutes away from their destination he moved in on her. His breath warmed her cheek. "You don't mind," he said, and turned her face up.

She did mind…but she didn't. And his lips closed over hers and he said, "I like you very much, more than I ever wanted to like anyone."

"Don't do me any favors," she said, and tried to pull away.

"Please," he said, and it was impossible to resist that gentle supplication. She gave him her lips, was with it all the way.

The taxi came to a stop. "Oh," Steve said, and let her go. He took out his wallet.

"*Gracias*," the driver said, giving them both an interested and sympathetic look. "*Buenas noches*, Senor, Senora."

The elevator rode them up.

"Call you in the morning," Steve said.

"All right."

She took a quick bath and then got into bed. There was only one more day in Madrid. After that, Steve Connaught would be only a memory. He was a big talker. And hers was a life in which people came and went. Nothing had permanence. You chose it, she told herself, as she pulled the covers up in the chilled, air-conditioned room. You have no one to blame but yourself.

CHAPTER 7

It was totally unexpected to hear from Constant Comstock the next morning.

He rang at shortly after nine o'clock, excusing himself for having possibly waked her. "It's all right," she said. "I got up a short while ago."

"May I take you to breakfast?" he asked.

"Oh?" She was, to say the least, astonished. What could he want? But she said yes, since her woman's curiosity was aroused, and they agreed to meet downstairs in the hotel lounge within the hour.

He was there when she went in, after having left her room key with Miguel. He stood up and she thought, he's a distinguished man, pleasantly ugly, quite sexual, and with a great deal of authority.

They went to Lhardy's, and of course it was brunch. *Cocido madrileno*, a delicious stew made of chick peas, potatoes, chopped meat, sausage and fatty bacon, headily seasoned, and afterwards a smooth, cool *flan* with dark coffee. With coffee Constant Comstock suggested cognac.

When the amber liquid was brought, she sipped it, waiting for the meaning of his visit. And as he lit his cigarette, his eyes reflective and ruminating, she knew he was about to come to the point. He leaned forward and asked her if she had enjoyed her meal.

"Yes, it was excellent. Thank you."

"It's a good old place. And I was glad to be here with you. You're the kind of woman who seems to know how to take care of herself." His eyes looked admiringly, but without flirtation, into hers. "More than that," he added, "you seem to be someone who can take care, not only of herself, but of others as well. Pretty women are everywhere. But pretty women with character are not to be found on every street corner."

"It's my job to take care of people," she said, faintly irritated. What was the purpose of this meeting? She was suddenly a little wearied of Constant Comstock's didactic manner. She wondered if Steve had called her, wanting breakfast.

"So you're off to the Costa del Sol tomorrow morning."

"Yes, I'm leaving at ten."

"I hope it will be a good trip."

"I'm sure it will."

"You said you were flying to Malaga?"

"Yes, and then spend a night in Torremolinos. Then hire a car for the rest of the time."

"You'll hit the high spots? Cordoba, Granada, Seville?"

"Right. In Seville I'll pick up an Interline courtesy flight to Lisbon and then be on the job again on the return flight to the States."

"I see." He smiled, said that it was a most pleasant itinerary and then let the bomb drop. "Richard would love a trip like that."

And before she could collect her wits, he added, "You see, I expect some trouble. With Richard's mother. And my heart is set on keeping the boy out of it. I'm sure you can understand. It's ridiculous of me to ask you this favor. But you see, I've been wondering if you'd be willing to take Richard with you. I know it's asking quite a lot. But—"

He saw her raised hand and her shocked look. He went on talking, the red flush warming his cheekbones. "It's an incredible imposition," he was saying. "Yet it would…help the boy and help me. Keep Richard from the line of fire, which is sure to come. Oh, I know it would cut into your holiday, but—"

She stared at him. He wanted her to take Richard with her? She could scarcely believe her ears. "Trouble," he said again, hurriedly.

"Lisa will be sure to…I don't want that child in the middle of it. Of course you can say no, the hell with it. I'm, in effect, throwing myself on your…mercy, good-will."

He sat back, tapping his fingers on the table top. "I suppose it's way out of line," he said at last. "Forgive me, it was a stupid request. Of course you want your time to yourself."

And she found herself saying, to her own surprise," I wouldn't mind taking Richard with me, Mr. Comstock. I think it would be rather nice to discover the countryside with your nephew. Admittedly it wasn't what I had in mind, but just the same…"

"You mean, you're not saying no?" His face lightened. "You'd be willing?"

I must be crazy, she thought, as she discussed what clothing Richard would need for the trip. "Shorts, shirts, sneakers."

"I think you're wonderful," Constant Comstock said, ordering another round of cognacs. "How can I possibly thank you?"

When he left her off at the hotel, Miguel, frowning, said, "This is a mistake, Senorita. The other man…he's more for you."

"*What?*"

"This one. He's too old."

She laughed. "Miguel, the man I was with this morning is the uncle of the little boy. He's very much married, and to a woman who looks like Helen of Troy. You're barking up the wrong tree. Have you seen Steve?"

"On the terrace. He has been calling your room, paging you, and walking up and down the whole place like a caged tiger. Now he's outside, probably drinking it up, like a fish. He loves you."

"Don't be ridiculous."

"No no. Believe me."

"You're sure he's outside?"

"Yes, drinking hard."

"Okay, I'll find him."

"Senorita, be kind. He has it bad."

"Oh, shut up, Miguel. Did I tip you today?"

"No."

"Then here," She shoved some paper money across the counter.

"I don't want your money, darling." Bur he took it.

"See you later."

"Remember. Be nice to that man."

Steve, looking dour, was drinking martinis. He looked up as she approached and said sourly, "Where the hell have you been?"

"Are you your brother's keeper?"

"Don't give me any of that lip. Go away. Who needs you? I'm occupied."

He was rather looped.

She sat down. "I have a companion for my Andalusian trip," she told him. "May I sit down?"

"You've already sat."

"May I have something to drink?"

He waved a finger at a waiter who came running over. "Ask the lady what she wants," he said, his voice slurred.

"A dry martini," Kelly said, and when the waiter, grinning, went away, she leaned toward Steve. "Did you hear what I said?"

"No."

"Richard's uncle wants me to take him to Andalusia."

"Fine," he said. "Just what I needed. The three of us."

"What do you mean by *that?*"

"Did you think you were sluffing me off?" he demanded, and suddenly his voice wasn't so blurred any more. "I have a ten o'clock flight to Malaga tomorrow morning. Did you imagine you were going to throw me off just like that?"

"You mean—"

"You sound like a soap opera," he said. " 'You mean? Am I to understand, sir, that—' "

"Screw it,' Steve," she said, and asked him again. "You're going to Andalusia too?"

"We can have breakfast on the plane," he said. "I've arranged for a car to take us to the airport. And a transfer on the other end. Be ready at eight-thirty."

"You didn't think to ask me, did you?"

"Why? If I want to go to Andalusia, I can damned well go. Do I have to ask your permission?"

"Certainly not. I hope Richard and I will run across you occasionally. Have a nice time, Steve."

"I said I'd arranged for transportation for us," he said. "It will be the three of us now. Naturally I had opted for two of us, but that seems to be the impossible dream. All right, we'll be Mama and Papa to a ten year old." That aggressive jaw jutted. "Don't you know when something's exactly *right* between two people? You won't find many men, Kelly, who feel the same way about you I do."

"We've only just met each other," she said shakily.

"Cut it," he said irritably. "Finish your drink, please, because since we're leaving tomorrow morning I want you to call that number."

"What number?"

"The Nascimentos."

"What for?"

"I want to go and see them."

"Why, Steve?"

"I'm curious about them. It's an idea, that's all."

"All right. It's just that it seems like ancient history by now." But she fished out the piece of paper with their telephone number, and when the call went through she asked to speak to Senor Nascimento.

"One moment, please."

There was a short silence and then the man's voice came on again. "Sorry, no answer."

"No answer? Isn't this Senor Nascimento's home?"

"This is the Hotel Independa."

"Where are you located?"

This time the voice was bored. "In the Calle del Sacramento. Numero—"

"Thank you very much."

Steve got out his guidebook. "Okay, it's in an old, illustrious quarter. Let's go."

The cab driver, when told of their destination, asked if they were headed for the Palacio de los Vargas.

"No, the Hotel Independa," Steve said, lighting a cigar.

"Ah, *si.*"

They drove through narrow Madrid streets and broad avenidas, palm-lined, with outdoor cafes at regular intervals. The sun burned everything; the sky was without clouds. Their driver obligingly pointed out places of interest. "The Cathedral of San Isidro," he told them, and later, "The Madrid Town Hall…this is beautiful, *si?* And look, the Plaza de la Villa, the work of Gomez de la Mora. Beautiful."

The cab driver hung his head out.

"Beautiful," he said again, and then just around the corner from this landmark was the Calle del Sacramento, with its Palacio de los Vargas.

The taxi came to a stop in front of an elaborate building, whose canopy bore the insignia Hotel Independa.

"Estan, Senor, Senora."

Steve paid him and they got out.

It was a rather plush hotel, with front gardens and a cool, expensive look. Inside, the lobby was dim and louvred; to the clerk at the desk Steve said, "I'm here to see Senor Nascimento."

"Pronto."

The desk clerk went to a telephone. Steve lit a cigar as they waited. "What are you going to say to them?" Kelly asked curiously, and Steve, raising an eyebrow, smiled. "I really hadn't given it much thought."

But the question was academic. After a moment or two the clerk hung up the phone. He walked back to them. "I am sorry, but Senor and Senora Nascimento have left the hotel."

"When?"

"Two hours ago, I was told."

"You're sure of that?"

"Certainly, Senor."

"What's their forwarding address?"

The clerk, a little flustered, checked a register. "I have none listed," he said.

"You're sure of that?"

"But…yes, I am sorry, Senor."

"You have no idea where they've gone?"

"No. No idea. There is no—"

"Why are you pursuing this?" Kelly asked him, as they walked out to the street again.

"I don't like unfinished stories."

"I don't either. I wonder where they went?"

"Maybe back with the return flight. Let's go back to the hotel and check last evening's passenger list."

When they were again at the Hotel Fenix Kelly called the airline. But the Nascimentos hadn't been booked on the ITA list for the evening before. "Okay, so it's a dead end," Steve said. "By this time I've lost interest, anyway. There are better things to do."

"Such as?"

"We could lie down and rest."

"If you're that tired, go ahead."

"I didn't mean alone, Kelly."

"Whatever you hear about us girls," she said, "don't believe a whole lot of it."

"I was afraid of that." He sighed. "Okay, then, let's take off for the Ermita de San Antonio. I understand there are some Goya frescoes there."

"Where is it?"

He consulted a notebook. "Paseo de la Florida." He went to the curb and held up a hand.

"Steve, it's not very far from here. We can walk. Do you own stock in cab companies?"

"How would I know where the damned place was?"

"You have a big-shot complex," she told him. "All the time taxis. Champagne for breakfast. Dollar cigars."

"So sue me."

She laughed, out of pleasure and contentment. Arm in arm they wandered through the old church, with its brilliant art works, the Goya frescoes as sublime as anything that artist had ever done. Afterwards they went to the Sabatini Gardens and then had drinks at a small, dark *posada* with vaulted brick ceilings. Candles flickered in the dim light; there was no air conditioning, but the thick stone walls kept out the heat.

A man whose long, sensitive fingers plucked at the strings of his guitar sang. Not tenor, not baritone, but somewhere in between.

"Yo te amo…bellaza…querida…"

The purple flowers, in bowls on the table tops, had a foresty scent. The candles lit the dark.

CHAPTER 8

The little Caravelle, with its tear-shaped windows, left Madrid at ten A.M., arriving an hour later at Malaga. The air of the Costa del Sol was clear and soft. Richard, lugging his suitcase, trudged through Customs and refused help from Steve. "I can manage," he said stoutly.

Their transfer took them, in short order, to the Hotel Pez Espada in Torremolinos, a half hour's drive. It was at the water's edge, and the Mediterranean was like glass, a clear, limpid blue. "Just like Miami," Richard said of the hotel, pinpointing it with deadly accuracy. Yet it was the last word in luxury and comfort, and the Costa del Sol was almost as charming as the French and Italian Rivieras, encompassing practically the whole of the Mediterranean coast frm Capo Gata to Tarifa.

It was picturesque still, with its fishing villages, subtropical valleys and high mountains that protected the coast from the chill of the hinterland. Starkly contrasting colors abounded; white-washed houses, agaves and prickly-pears, farmhouses and gay villages were set in an ambience of rich trees and luxuriant foliage. Torremolinos was the kick-off point from which the rest of Andalusia stretched, fascinating, sometimes somber, poor and arid in spots, incredibly brilliant with riches of the soil in others.

So said the guidebooks.

"We'll see," Steve said, lighting a cigar as they had drinks at an outdoor bar of the hotel.

The manager, Senor Manos, refused to accept payment for their cocktails. And when they went back to their rooms, both Kelly and Steve found a bottle of chilled champagne in a bucket. Kelly was used to such attentions; all airline employees received these courtesies. "You're, a good gal to know," Steve said.

In the afternoon they hired a car and driver and inside of twenty minutes were back in Malaga, a beautiful little town perched on a cliff, the outstanding feature of which was the famous lookout point of Balcon de Europa and which afforded a magnificent view of the sea and mountains.

Locked in all this beauty was a huge amphitheater down below, where the festival of the bulls was held. "Want to go to a bull-fight?" Steve asked Richard, and the boy's face paled.

"Do we have to?"

"No, Rich. First of all, Kelly would hate it. And I've never seen one that didn't churn up my guts."

"Oh, good. I like the music, of course, but—"

"The music is something, I have to agree. The Virgin of the Macarena. But the works are grim. We'll stay away from the blood sports, all right, Rich?"

"Yeah, I'm glad, Steve. Because…it's the horses, you know."

"It's the horses, yes. And everything else. We don't like stuff like that, do we?"

"Not me."

"Me either."

There were some gypsies. Not beautiful girls or women, but with a certain charm, in their tatterdemalion costumes, their strong arms raised over their heads, flashing their castanets. Pictures were taken. "This will go in my memoirs," Richard said.

They were driven back to the hotel, arriving at four o'clock, and then they got into their bathing suits and went down to the sea. There was only one other guest there, a middle-aged man, still white in the torso, asleep on a beach chair. They lay and turned their faces up to the sun. And fell asleep. Steve woke first, nudging Kelly with a foot.

"Turn over," he ordered. "Or you'll be a lobster."

Obediently, she changed position. Then fell asleep again.

When she woke next, Steve and Richard were tossing a big, red and blue beach ball back and forth. She watched them, a hand shading her eyes. She was conscious of a great sense of peace, of things being exactly as they should be, with the man and the boy, companionable, batting the ball back and forth. And the warm, golden afternoon.

They stayed until the sky purpled, then trudged back across the mauve-colored sand and back to their rooms. "We'll meet in the lounge at eight," Steve said, and they separated. Kelly crawled into bed for an hour or so, then got up, took a bath and got into a spectacular outfit. She was rewarded by a glint in Steve's eyes. Even Richard remarked on her splendor.

"That's a nice thing," he said, fingering a fold of her gown. "It looks Arabian."

"It is. I bought it in Morocco. It's a djellabah."

The gazpacho was cold and pungent, the beef rare and tender. It was almost midnight when they went upstairs. Richard's eyes were glazed and Kelly was half asleep.

They saw the boy to his room and Steve said, "Now how about going out on the town?"

"Are you kidding? I can scarcely keep my eyes open."

He grinned. "Me too. Anyway, there isn't anything around here. Just other hotels like this one. Grossingertype nightclubs. Just as well. We have to get an early start tomorrow. Be ready at eight."

"At *eight?*"

"Sure. It's a long drive to Cordoba. We want to be there by at least three o'clock. And I'm the one who has to get up *really* early. To rent a car for the trip. So the least you can do is be ready to go at around nine or so."

"I didn't think we'd have to start that early, Steve."

"Oh, stop playing on my sympathies. Kelly?"

"Yes?"

"I like you."

"That's a good thing to know."

"Don't be flippant. If you could manage to unfreeze a little, you think you could manage a good night kiss?"

"Go to bed and sleep it off," she said, fishing for her key.

"Not yet. Look at me."

"Oh, for heaven's sake."

"I'm waiting."

She dropped her keys and both of them bent to pick them up. Heads were bumped and then the next thing she knew she was in Steve Connaught's arms. "That was A OK," he said, after they kissed. "Thank you very much. And now close your little eyes and go to sleep. Morning will be here before you know it."

He pushed her into her room and she closed the door on his satisfied, smiling face. Leaning against the door, she thought, it's too good to be true. There must be a snag somewhere. Things like this just didn't happen…

The wide, cool bed was heaven, and she turned luxuriously, remembering the kiss and earlier, the fresh air, the sea, the peach-colored sand. And then she drowned in sleep, as the waves washed over her, the salty, sun-drenched waters of the Mediterranean, enclosing her in a kind of tender womb.

• • •

The alarm rang and then it was time to be up and going again. Packing, shoving garments hastily into her suitcase, she bathed and dressed. Steve rang her at a quarter to nine.

"Of course I'm up," she said crossly. "I'll be downstairs in fifteen minutes."

"Good girl. Richard's been awake since I guess dawn."

"Is he down there?"

"He's eating. Sausages and eggs and now he's on his third coke."

"For heaven's sakes, see that he drinks some milk," she said, and rang off.

It was so nice, she thought, joining them. Like a family. "Good morning, Kelly," Richard said amiably, sliding toward the wall so that she could sit next to him in, the booth. "You look nice in pants."

"She sure does," Steve said appreciatively. "She's a limber wench. I never did like fat women."

"Both of you shut up and stop eyeing me. I'm still half asleep. Some holiday this is. Up with the sparrows. I might as well be working."

• • •

The miles flew by, golden kilometers under a burning sun. Small villages lay sleepy in the summer somnolence. "Is this a *ciudad?*" Richard asked innumerable times. Sometimes it was; just as often it was a small *pueblo.*

They stopped off for coffee and the bathroom at several places en route, and reached their destination at just short of three o'clock. Cordoba was a splendid city, on the main Madrid-Cadiz national highway, at a height of about three hundred feet above sea level. Richard read them the particulars from his guidebook.

" 'Cordoba has a population of about 250,000 inhabitants and is one of the oldest cities in Spain, dating to prehistoric times, roughly, around the year 152 A.D.' "

He raised his head. "Jaysus, that's old, isn't it?"

"Richard, will you try to refine your language, just a *little?*"

"Oh. Sorry." He bent to his guidebook again. "Anyway. It became a Roman municipality and was granted the status of Colonia Patricia, as capital of lower Spain. Influential in the fortunes of the Empire were its native Seneca, the philosopher,

Lucanus, who composed the poem 'Pharsalia,' and Hosius, head of the Nicene Council."

"Thanks for the info," Steve drawled. "Now I know exactly where we stand."

"It's super, isn't it? What are we going to do when we get to the hotel?"

"Eat."

"What else?"

"Then sleep. We'll save the Mosque for tomorrow. All right, this afternoon we'll-hack around and take a gander at the Castle, the Montmayor. And, let's say, the Calle de las Flores and the Capuchin Monastery. We ought to work in the Tower of la Malmuerta. But I want all tomorrow morning for the Mosque. That's really supposed to be something."

● ● ●

The Hotel Cordoba Palace, deluxe and with a swimming pool in emerald gardens, was comfortably air-conditioned. They rested in their rooms for an hour, then met for a late lunch in the Senecan Room, after which they followed Steve's itinerary. Everything was white-washed, with inner courtyards in which the purple bougainvillea bloomed around marble columns and burbling fountains.

Later in the afternoon they drove to Montoro, on the Guadalquivir, with its beautiful churches and convents, and then went on to Almodovar and Pala del Rio, the latter rich in orange groves.

When it came time for dinner they were footsore and weary, but richly rewarded. A quick bath and a short rest brought them all together again at a quarter to ten, when the dining room of the hotel opened.

They ate outside, under the stars. There was a four piece combo and a singer with a melting voice.

"*…Guadalajara, gaudalajara, guadalajara…*"

The lanterns lit the water with their blue and red lights. The sky was dusky, the air clear and crisp. The heat of the day had given way to the cool of an Andalusian night. Richard fell asleep suddenly, his head falling, without warning, into his dessert, a strawberry *flan*.

"Oh?" He pulled himself up. "I guess I must have dozed off."

There was caramel custard on his nose, his forelock and the tip of his chin.

"It's bedtime for you," Kelly said, wiping his face and forehead with a napkin.

"I'm not tired," he protested.

"Don't be an idiot. You're alseep on your feet," Steve said.

"We're going places," Steve said, when Kelly came down again after taking Richard to his room.

"I'm going to bed."

"No you're not."

"Steve, I'm really pooped."

"You'll wake up again. It's only just past midnight. I found out a really picturesque place to go. The two of us. Mommy and Daddy on a night out."

"Really? And I suppose, even if you get me home at four in the morning, you'll want me to be on tap at eight o'clock."

"But Kelly, you're a healthy young girl."

"I don't know for how long. At the rate you've got me going. I had envisioned a lazy holiday in Andalusia. This has been anything but that. You're a slave driver."

"Finish your cigarette. There's this interesting night club. Come on, let's go."

"Do we have to?"

"Yes, I was told it's very much out of the way and no American ever went there."

"Leave it to you to set a precedent. What is this place?"

"It's called El Toro. It's on the Calle Basura. A ghastly section, apparently. We might both be knifed. Except, don't worry, *I* can take care of you. What's the name of this city?"

"Cordoba." She laughed. "If this is Tuesday, it must be Cordoba."

"That's right, Cordoba. And one of the stellar matadors these days is El Cordobes. According to Felipe, he frequents El Toro. I don't go for bullfights, but matadors have a certain glitter."

"Do you have any idea how sleepy I am?"

"You're young! Art is long and life is fleeting. Let's go, girl. I'll let you stay in bed later tomorrow. We're spending a whole other day here. Okay?"

•••

El Toro was indeed in a questionable section of the city.

Their taxi driver pulled a face. "I could get a dagger in my back," he objected. "There are better places…in the Florida quarter…"

"Be a sport," Steve said, opening his wallet. He pulled out some notes. "Will this help?"

"It won't help a dead man."

"We want to go there. We were told that El Cordobes shows up once in a while."

"El Cordobes isn't afraid of a knife in the ribs."

But in the end he took them there.

It was the Hell's Kitchen of the city. Dark, dingy, with a forsaken look, the street was like a waterfront area, with long, cavernous alleyways and litter and dung in the gutters. The driver let them out as soon as he had collected his fare, and then sped away quickly.

But inside, the *posada* was rather cheerful. The lights were fairly bright, once they went down a long flight of worn wooden steps, and the clientele, if inclined to be rough types, were amiable and clearly enjoying themselves.

There were, of course, necks craned at the entry of the Americans, and one or two resentful looks came their way. Steve hastened to say that Felipe, at the Hotel Granada Palace, had sent them, and then there was a warm welcome.

"Ah, Felipe…a good friend of mine!"

They were seated, and after a while, as the manager went from table to table explaining that these people were friends of friends of his, their presence was accepted.

"Do you like it?" Steve asked, as they drank.

"I wouldn't recommend it to my friends, but yes, it's interesting," she admitted.

After a while a singer stood in a hot spotlight, an ugly but fascinating-looking woman. She did a rather suggestive number. At its end there was coarse laughter and riotous hand-clapping, but then she sang a mournful Catalan ballad, haunting and melancholy. Kelly saw a big, sweating man with a ruined face wiping his eyes at the end of it. And this time the applause was quiet and restrained.

They were there for a little over an hour, and just as they were about to leave, a tall, ginger-haired young man with a wide, sweet mouth and superb white teeth came down the stairs. There was instantly a kind of bedlam. Shouts went up.

"*Ole…ole…ole…*"

It was the matador.

The manager rushed forward, kissed the young man's hand, and bowed. Then he turned and held both hands high above his head.

"*Senor y Senores…El Cordobes…*"

"*Bienvenido!*" the guests at the tables cried, getting to their feet.

The bullfighter, simple, shirt-sleeved, extraordinarily handsome, scattered pesos to the waiters. There was a beautiful girl with him. He sat quietly at a table, murmuring to the girl with him.

"I told you," Steve said. "Didn't I tell you he came here?"

She was pleased for Steve. He was so set up. So triumphant. All men were little boys at heart.

She glanced across at the toreador. He was rather haunting. That boy faced the bulls, with their pronged horns, and he looked like a Richard of ten years hence. Gentle, with a sweep of reddish blond hair, blue eyes that were without guile.

Outside was darkness, quite frightening, and elongated shadows. Luckily, a cab drove up, letting off a party of working people, and they got in. It was almost four o'clock when Kelly pulled the sheets back.

She fell asleep remembering the plaintive ballad the woman had sung.

El manzano…la cantilena…y el oro…

CHAPTER 9

Faithful to his word, Steve had let Kelly sleep. It was almost eleven when she woke. The waiter in the dining room served her, saying that he understood that the Senor and Senora had gone last night to El Toro.

"Yes, it was a very unusual place," she said. "The matador was there."

"El Cordobes. Ah…" He kissed his fingers. "A wonderful boy…you know he gives to the poor. Much money. He comes from the poor and he has never forgotten."

His shoulders went up. "He is not Manolete, of course. Not the same style. But he is brave, very brave."

"He must be. Have you seen Mr. Connaught this morning?"

"Yes, he and the boy are in the back, in the pool."

So it was to be a leisurely morning after all. She finished, and then went back to her room, where she changed into a bikini. And then joined her friends.

Steve was at the edge of the board, flexing his muscles. He didn't see her. He stood there for another moment, then took a dive. She stood looking down at him as his arms cut the water.

"Well done," she said.

"Ah…" He looked up at her, his dark hair wet and gleaming. "So you decided to get up at long last."

"I've wanted a sleep like that for the past few days."

"So you feel okay?"

"Wonderful."

"Then come on in," he said. "The water's fine."

She went down the flight of submerged steps and joined him. "Race you to the other end," he said.

They got to the finish line at the same time. Richard was there, sitting at the edge of the pool with some other American children. "Hey," he said cheerily. "Isn't this great?"

She pushed back her wet hair. "Um hum. Did you have milk for breakfast?"

"Yeah, Steve made me drink a whole gallon, I guess."

"That's a good Steve."

And then they lay, tanning, on deck chairs. There was an ineffable breeze, rendering the tropical sun bearable. "You look gorgeous with a tan," Steve murmured, opening an eye. "You're so nice-looking, Kelly."

She didn't say anything, only smiled. The cries of the children, the wafting of the breeze, the wonderful, beneficent sun and the man beside her.

This is Eden, she thought, closing her eyes again. It's Paradise. If she died right now, at this moment, it would be all right. And she remembered the song again.

El manzano, la cantilena, y el oro…

The apple trees, the singing, and the gold.

• • •

After a light lunch they left the hotel in the car.

"Where are we headed for?" Richard asked interestedly.

"The Alcazar."

"What's that?"

"Take a look at your guidebook."

"Okay."

Richard fished out his paraphernalia.

"Ah yes," he said, crackling the stiff paper. "The Mosque is the crowning achievement of local Caliphate art. Begun by Abd el Rahman in the mid-eighth century, it was successively enlarged during the—"

"Little friend, read to yourself, okay?" Steve asked, pained, and Richard subsided, his lips moving as he pored over the literature in his lap.

Of course they walked first, through the *callejas*, the crooked, winding streets which were steeped in the essence of bygone Cordoba. Even their names were fascinating: los Rincones de Oro, La Luna, the Cuenta de Pero Mato.

And, unforgettable sight, the Puerta de Sevilla, near the monument to Ibn Hazm, with its dazzling view of the city walls.

They stopped off for a second breakfast at a small but superb *fonda* near the Montmayor, where they had a delicious paella and one of the chilled, delicious white wines of the Aguilar de la Frontera.

"Are we going to the Alcazar now?" Richard asked.

"Just as soon as Kelly finishes her cigarette."

"I'm ready," she said, and stubbed it out.

The Alcazar was stupefying, its central dome of the Mihrab chapel one of the wonders of the world. It was Richard who pointed out, guidebook in hand, that the Mosque had the curious feature of facing southwards instead of east.

It was a formidable palace, Moorish, and at this off season, deserted. The entry fee was a few pesetas apiece and once inside its labyrinthine vastness, one had the feeling of being buried alive. If there had been other visitors, it might have been less eerie. But there were none.

The three of them were its only occupants, and their voices echoed in the great, vaulted corridors, which were arched in the Mauresque manner, striped in orange and sand-color, like some exotic desert tent, like a strange caravansery that went on, literally, forever, an infinity of chambers that stretched ahead without, it seemed, any end to its arched convolutions.

"The mysterious East," Steve murmured.

"I have a Western mentality," Kelly told him. "This kind of thing makes my blood run cold."

The Alcazar was like a huge beehive, its parallel chambers reaching as far as the eye could see and even further. Columns rose, disappeared, and other columns took their place. You could circle around endlessly, or so it appeared to the confused eye. Richard, in fact, was weaving his way in and around pillars, calling, "Hoo hoo…hoo hoo," and listening to his voice ringing out in answer. Kelly asked him, after a while, please to stop, and he did. For which one was grateful; it was spooky enough without *that*.

"Give me a good old Gothic cathedral any time," she said, and Steve told her she was narrow in her outlook. Then he confessed he felt the same way. Of course it was magnificent in its bizarre, Oriental way, and the central dome of the Mihrab chapel was a masterpiece of tessellated design, each perfect tile forming an exquisitely-colored kaleidoscope of the most fabulous and inventive patterns.

But it was pagan, was more fanciful than the Western mind could tolerate without some uneasiness. There was a kind of cruelty in its primigenial tribute to Saracen worship; there was no recognizable spirituality here, no feeling of mercy, peace, or deliverance.

Steve was briefing her from his own guidebook.

"Built from the eighth to the tenth centuries," he read. "Yes, Richard's right. Islamic doctrine dictates that places of worship face the east, but this doesn't. It faces south. Funny, I wonder why?"

He looked up. "Those alternating orange and yellow patterns striping the arches are called *voussoirs*."

He leaned against a pillar.

"Roman, Visigothic and Caliphate art are combined in an architectural melange. The original choir-stalls and the sixteenth century Gothic-Renaissance cathedral section."

He stopped reading.

"This lousy fine print. My eyes aren't what they used to be. Where the hell *is* the center of this chamber of horrors, anyway?"

"There isn't any. It's like time. An eternal circle, no beginning and no end. We're lost forever. This will be our tomb."

"Then let's die happy," he said, reaching for her hand. "Let's make love, before hunger and thirst drive all such thoughts from our minds."

"You are really a nut, Steve."

"I'm a full-blooded American male and I have you in my power, my dear. Don't fight it, lass. *C'est plus fort que—*"

"If you think that, you don't know me," she said, fending him off. "I've been taking care of myself for a long time. Did I tell you I know judo? Come here, Steve, and I'll show you a few throws."

He groaned. "I was afraid of a lot of things, but I never thought about that."

"Now you know."

"Tell me about your brother," he said.

"How do you know it was a brother?"

"Because you handle men so well. So it's a brother, not a sister."

"It *was* a brother."

"It *was?*"

His eyes questioned her.

"Yes. Lewis. He's dead. Vietnam. He was a photographer. He got killed on the Pleine des Jarres. Just taking pictures, you understand. For *Life* magazine. He was a nice boy. We were quite close."

"Christ, I'm sorry."

"It's happening all the time," she said brightly.

"You poor kid."

"I've learned to live with it. I don't know about my mother and father."

"I never guessed," he said miserably. "When I said that about Scarsdale…"

"It doesn't matter where. Don't look like that, Steve. It's been absorbed, taken into account, resigned to. We all have our little troubles."

The silence was like a weight on them. It was almost cold. The ponderous stone carapace of the Mosque shut out the Cordoban heat, shut out the bright, steaming day, shut out the world. When she shivered, Steve put an arm around her.

"It is kind of nasty in here," he said. "Like a lost world. Like—"

He stopped talking suddenly.

They had both slowed up. There was now an immense silence, no ringing footfalls, no resounding voices echoed back. There was just that ghastly, cold silence. It was really like being enclosed in a tomb, like breathing the dank air of death, a final and ineluctable end to sunlight and beauty and laughter.

"Where's Richard?" Steve asked.

"Just up ahead, I expect."

Steve put his hand on one of the great blocks of stone that was part of a pillar, and called.

"Richard."

There was no answer.

He called again.

"Richard!"

There was still no response.

And Kelly felt her flesh crawl.

"Call him again," she said sharply.

"Jesus Christ," Steve said angrily. "Where did that little bastard go to?" He dropped her hand and began walking rapidly through the corridors. "Come on, let's see where the little jerk is."

And then they were walking faster, almost running.

"Steve, why are you so—?" Kelly asked.

He didn't bother to answer. Suddenly it was a nightmare; those interminable corridors, the pillars flashing by, striped and now quite hideous, as they plunged down the series of archways, their heels clashing against the marble underfoot.

It was like…we should have a compass, Kelly thought…like running, as you did in horrible dreams, through eternity, never being able to catch up with what you wanted to find…whatever it was.

This incredible, abandoned place…like hell, perhaps, like the underworld. And then, blessedly, there was an end to the apparently endless corridors. Through an open doorway, a mere slit in the wall, the green of grass was framed, like a glorious picture, dead ahead. Steve shot through the narrow aperture and after him, Kelly. It was like being given life again…to see the sky, to feel the warmth of the day:

Seated outside on the grass, reading studiously, his face intent, Richard sat, legs splayed, looking peaceful and content.

"Damn you," Steve barked. "Didn't you hear us screeching for you?"

The boy looked up.

"Wha'?"

Steve swore under his breath. "Get up and say you're sorry," he thundered. "When you're with me you stay with me, is that understood?"

"But—"

"Apologize!"

There was a stunned silence. Then Richard, eyes wide, scrambled up. "I'm sorry if—"

"All right, all right! Don't ever do that again. Wander away… who do you think you are, you little joker?"

"What did I *do?*"

"You left us! We were yelling for you! Who gave you permission to—"

Something shone in the boy's eyes, and it wasn't hurt or resentment, Kelly saw. It was a kind of slowly dawning admiration. He didn't mind the scolding. In fact, he liked it. A man's authority, a man's anger.

"I didn't realize," he said. "Gee, I just didn't think."

"Well, from now on you think," Steve said grimly. "I mean what I said, Rich. We're responsible for you. And you're to remember that."

"I will, Steve."

"Okay. Now let's get away from this crazy place."

• • •

They had lunch at La Rambla, where there was a gift shop with beautiful pottery, and later went on to Castro de Rio and Pozoblanco. Richard made a trip to the bathroom and Kelly asked Steve why he had been so upset at the boy's disappearance in the Mosque.

"Nothing happened," she said. "Yet you made a real Federal case out of it."

"It's over with now. Let's forget about it."

"Uh uh. What was all the shouting about?"

He lit a cigar. "Okay, you might as well know. Richard's a very rich boy. Through an inheritance from his paternal grandmother. Grape nuts, or something similar. There's a lot of money riding on that kid."

"How do you know all this?"

"I make it my business to find out things."

"Why? Who are you?"

"What does it matter?"

"Steve, you're unfair. You tell me these things and I'm supposed to sit back and smile nicely. I want to know."

He looked away, puffed on his cigar and leaned back. "Let it go."

"No. When Richard disappeared, you thought someone had—"

He didn't say anything.

"You thought someone had…taken him."

She knew then; she had a flash of insight. She should have guessed it before. "Why, you're watching out for Richard," she said. "It wasn't coincidence. You didn't just *happen* to be on the same plane with him. You came over with him. I wondered about that. A child under ten is always accompanied by a stewardess; that's a rule of the airline. Over ten is in a different category, but just the same…and if you're right, if Richard is a very wealthy boy, no one would take chances with such a child. So you came along to keep an eye on him. Why? Whom do you represent?"

"A relative," he said reluctantly. "Let it go at that."

"Constant. Richard's uncle."

"Let it lay, Kelly."

"Was it Constant?"

Even if he had wanted to answer, it was too late. Richard trotted back to his chair again. Could he have another coke, please? Kelly caught Steve's eye and he grinned companionably… but secretively. Why, he must be a private eye! A man who led a dangerous life.

But it didn't change things. Whatever he was, whoever he was, she was in love with him. So much for upbringing. For the first time in her life she was a captive. The lessons she had learned at Mother's knee wouldn't help her now. The cigarette Steve lit for her wavered between trembling fingers, and she might be making the biggest mistake of her life, but she was very much in love with that man. Everything else…career, aspirations, the dream of a quiet, dignified life drew a big, fat blank.

He saw it in her eyes; she knew that. And saw his gratification. Resented it, but could do nothing about it. A furtive life…that was what he led, and she had guessed it almost from the beginning. A man who spied on people, who looked into peepholes.

"Could I please have another coke?" Richard asked.

CHAPTER 10

Echoes. Resounding echoes. Red stripes on a vaulted ceiling. Ahead stretched infinity, in its awfulness, its finality. Why am I alone? Kelly thought, turning to look for Steve, holding out a hand, absently, for Richard.

But they weren't there.

Not Steve, not Richard.

Then, she told herself reasonably, they were just beyond the next arch. She had been so busy looking at the brilliant tiles on the walls that she hadn't noticed. They had just gone on ahead, that was all.

Confidently, she walked quickly ahead, was in another corridor. Another corridor just like the last one. They were all the same. They were repetitions. Ad infinitum. Forever!

Because there was no end, of course.

No beginning?

No.

And no end.

I hate this place, she thought. I don't want to be here.

"Where are you?" she asked her friends.

She walked ahead, gaining the corridor beyond. They must be here, of course.

No, they were not. They were not! There was no one there, not the sound of a voice, not the ghost of a whisper. Her footfalls echoed on the marble tile of the floor, rang out loudly.

She was alone. They had left her. She was alone.

And exactly where? Because where was the end and where the beginning of this maze? Where had it started? To where did it lead?

This is horrible, she thought, in the terrible grip of claustrophobia. I can't possibly stand this.

She put out her arms, as if to push away the walls, as if, like Sampson, she could bring the pillars crashing down, see the hideous tomb of Abd el Rahman break into ruins, show the bright blue of the sky outdoors.

A bird flew by. She ducked, filled with horror. A bird? And yet she loved them, loved all wild creatures. The bird rushed past her, its wings almost tangling in her hair. The rushing sound of its flight filled her ears, deafening, and she caught sight of the eyes, cruel and intent. The eyes looked at her, calculating and savage, and then the bird soared up again, brushing against the vaulting of the ceiling, poised for further devastations.

She knew its plan. To destroy her. Yes, it was clear what the creature had in its mind. And then, with a caw of anger, it beat its wings and dive-bombed.

She screamed.

"No…no…"

But the bird, in its swift, terrifying descent, plummeted down. She wound her hands round her head but, with a deafening rush of powerful wings, the eagle crashed down on her.

There was the slash of its talons. The blood poured down her forehead. The claws were intent on her eyes, tearing, tearing.

Her eyes!

The scream forced its way past her tight throat.

• • •

Steve woke up with a start.

What the hell was that? he thought.

Someone had screamed bloody murder.

He slid out of bed.

The *scream* died away.

At the interconnecting door he paused.

Had he been dreaming?

Everything was quiet now.

And then, suddenly, there was the repressed sound of sobbing, as if a child was on the other side of that door. A little girl…

Hell, that was Kelly.

He stood a minute, and then turned the doorknob.

She was curled up in the fetal position. In the dim light from outdoors he could see her shoulders shaking. She heard him come in, and gasped.

"Who's there?"

Her hands came away from her head.

"It's only me. I heard you."

"Oh. It's all right. It was only a dream."

"All right. Talk about it."

He sat down on the edge of the bed.

"No no, it's too stupid."

"Don't be a joker. What was this dream?"

She gave a shaky laugh. "Something about a big bird. It's insane. I love birds."

"What did the bird do?"

"It tried to…" She shuddered. "Yipes, I'm sorry," she said. "But it was rather disgusting."

"Tell me."

"I just wonder why we have such garbage in our minds," she said. "It was such an obscene dream. The bird was going for my eyes."

She laughed again, trembling in his arms.

"Imagine? My eyes, you understand."

"It was only a dream."

"Yeah, but why?"

"Atavism," he said. "We're what thousands of centuries have made us. We still have the primordial fears."

"I suppose."

He cradled her, and she was passive, quiescent. "It was that Mosque," she said finally. "That weird, bizarre place. That's something that gets to you."

"Yes, it was unpleasant, rather."

"Of course that was the reason for my rotten dream."

"I'm sure."

"I don't even like Spain much. It's another kind of civilization. It's alien to me, really."

"Sure. I understand."

He let her talk.

And at last she subsided.

"I'm all right now," she said. "You were very good to come to me."

"It wasn't altruism," he said. "If you haven't guessed by now, you're not as bright as I think you are."

She stiffened in his arms.

Finally she said, as if it were painful, "I like hearing that. But just the same. You understand…"

"Understand what?"

"I don't…I mean I can't…really, Steve, *can't*…"

She swallowed. "I mean, follow it up."

"Did you think I wanted to get into bed with you?" he asked.

"Oh, I just mean…"

"I do want to get into bed with you. But not like this. Kelly, for God's sake. I'm a man, I can always get girls…women…"

He put her away from him.

"What I'm trying to say is, I'm not out for an easy thing. They come a dime a dozen. I just want to tell you that hearing you cry out, knowing you had a need for someone and that I was there to supply that need. Why, that's the most beautiful thing I can think of. That I could come to you, hold you and comfort you. For now, that's the best, that's what I want, what I prize. I won't even kiss you. Give me your little hand, let me hold it to my heart. That's the sweet girl. You are a sweet girl, Kell. Nothing hard or brittle about you."

He put her hand to his chest.

"Christ, look what I found," he said huskily. "Look what I found right out of the blue."

Then he got up.

"I'm right next door," he reminded her. "So if there's anything else—we could, of course, play double solitaire if you can't sleep."

And then she was able to laugh. "I'll sleep," she said.

"Sure?"

"Yes. And thank you, Steve."

He went out and she heard him moving in the next room. It was so reassuring. I never felt alone before, she thought, drifting off. But of course she had been alone. She'd had fun, but—

Look what I found, Steve had said, and she said the same words to herself.

Look what she found.

CHAPTER 11

Lisa Comstock, at the Hassler Hotel in Rome, placed a call to New York City. She was in bed and propped up on fat pillows. Everything she had on her body was hand-made…the nightgown and the bedjacket. Real silk, and the trim Brussels lace. There had never been a time when she had known anything else. She had been reared in luxury, first in a Palazzo in Florence and then, when she was a very small child, in Manhattan, on Park Avenue.

She had been eighteen when she married an extremely wealthy, older man, and she was the mother of a child whose inheritance was enormous. Richard's money was tied up in a trust fund, but it also provided handsomely for his mother until he reached the age of twenty-one.

She could come and go as she pleased; yet she was not a happy woman. She had been the deb of the year when she came out; now, at just past thirty, she saw her beauty dimming. There were small, fine lines at the corners of her eyes and her inky black hair sprouted an occasional gray strand. She spent several minutes every morning with an eyebrow tweezer, yanking them out and feeling the depression washing over her.

My God, people really did get old!

Like most young persons she had always thought simplistically; there were the young and there were the old. And now, only quite recently, she had begun to understand that there was no real division. You were young for a while and then you got older.

It had been an astonishing, shocking, almost obscene recognition. That she was destined to fall, some day, some hideous day, into the other category.

That one day she would be old.

To be old…

The thought kept her awake many nights, and so she had turned to liquor and sex when Lawrence had died. To quiet the tumult in her soul, to anesthetize herself. There were some things a person simply could not bear to dwell on. And so you did whatever was necessary. If it made you feel better it didn't matter what it was.

Hundreds of Manhattan men of sterling caliber would have married this widow in a minute for what she had to offer. But she didn't want to get married again. She wanted to *want* to, but she was a narcissist. Her only real concern was the care of her body, and the dread of its aging. She was a sick woman, but she didn't know it. She didn't know anything about herself.

The phone rang beside her bed.

"Your call to New York," the operator said. "Go ahead, please."

She spoke to Martha, the housekeeper. "Yes, I'm all right," she said. "Oh, I've had a cold, but it's going now. Martha, I'm leaving here and will be home on the ninth. My flight gets in at seven P.M. Have George be there, at the field. And I'd like Richard to be with him."

There was no immediate answer, and she frowned impatiently.

"Martha? Did you hear me?"

"But Richard is in Spain," the housekeeper said.

"What did you say?"

"He's in Madrid, with his uncle."

"*What?*" Lisa dragged herself up from the pillows. "You're not serious! I don't understand. In *Spain?*"

Then she started screeching. "How did…Who managed this? That wretched man…you mean he…"

She swung her legs out of the bed and reached for a gin bottle on a marble-topped table. Shaking, her fingers unscrewed the cover.

"Hello," she said. "Martha?"

"Yes, Mrs. Comstock."

"Hold on. Just a minute."

She picked up the glass, but her hand was shaking so badly that it fell to the floor and shattered with a tinkling sound. Damn it, she cried inwardly, and lifted the bottle to her lips.

Oh, God, how good that felt.

The liquor, warm and comforting, trickled down. It was so wonderful…

She took the phone again. "Now tell me," she said. "Tell me exactly what happened."

She listened, grimly, and when she hung up she got the operator again and had a call put through to Madrid.

"It's someone calling from Rome," the little Spanish girl said in a soft, tentative voice. Senor Comstock was reading in the library; he looked up, at first abstractedly, and then jumped up out of his chair.

"Rome?"

Aha, he thought. So she had found out. "It's all right, I'll get it," he said, and went over to the desk to pick up the extension.

"This is Constant Comstock," he said, his lips curved into a faint smile.

"This is Lisa. Where's my son?"

"Richard?"

"Where is he? Put him on instantly."

"I can't very well do that, Lisa."

Oh, how he was enjoying himself!

"Why not?" The woman's voice was harsh, uncontrolled.

"Because he isn't here."

There was a stunned silence, while he savored her shock and confusion. Then, "Isn't there? Where is he?"

"He's having a glorious holiday in Andalusia. With friends."

"Friends? What are you talking about? Are you crazy?"

"No, not at all. He's with good friends, very responsible people, and I'm sure he's having the time of his life."

"I don't believe you. I want to talk to him. Put him on!"

"I'm sorry, Lisa. You can't speak to him." He was regretful. "He's on the way to Seville. Is there something I can do for you, my dear?"

"Damn you. Don't give me that line of…How dare you do a thing like this? Send for him behind my back…how dare you?"

"Why, he's my nephew," he said, gently. "I'm fond of that boy. I thought it would be a pleasant holiday for him. Instead of being cooped up in New York with only servants for company. Surely you must agree I did right?"

"I'll…" Her voice broke. "You'll see, I'll have you locked up. This is—"

"This is only a very natural interest an uncle takes in a beloved nephew," Constant said, and his voice was like steel now. "And by the way, I feel for you, Lisa. That business in Rome must have been so very disturbing…"

She started to say something, choked, and then slammed down the receiver. Her sobs filled the room. I can't, she thought, reaching for the gin bottle. I can't stand my life…how could anyone stand this kind of life?

• • •

"Kelly?"

She was half asleep; she almost dropped the phone.

"Hum?"

"Kelly, are you there?"

"Who's this?" Her lips felt numb.

"Steve. Who do you think?"

"Oh, hello."

"Get up."

"What?"

"Honey, it's wearing on, almost ten. The dining room will close."

"Oh that's all right. I don't care."

"Listen, you get out of that bed," he said. "I'm telling you."

"Doesn't it mean anything to you that I'm tired?"

"What about me? I was kept up half the night by a hysterical female."

And then she remembered. Her voice softened; she turned over onto her back. "Oh, Steve, I'm sorry."

"Forget it. But honey, breakfast in half an hour. All right?"

"Yes, Steve."

"Don't go back to sleep. You won't, will you?"

"No, Steve."

"If you're not down in half an hour I'll come up and drag you down. Got that?"

"Yes, Steve."

• • •

Granada was hilly, precipitous, and very picturesque, particularly where it crossed through the Sierra de Agreda. The view when approaching the city was magnificent, with the white and jagged Sierra Nevada standing clear-cut against the horizon.

They had left Cordoba by the Roman Bridge over the Guadalquivir and passed the Seville Road, continuing through Torres Cabrera and Santa Cruz.

They came to the Alhambra Palace Hotel at just short of two o'clock in the afternoon. The hotel was really splendid, much larger than the others so far, and their rooms, again adjoining, looked out from terraces that were like cliff-dwelling quarters. There was a breathtaking view of the valley where white-washed houses with red tiled roofs clambered up and down the hills of Granada. Everything was blinding; the sun flashed brilliant and hot.

They had lunch right away and then started out adventuring. The main thoroughfare was the Calle de los Reyes Catolicos, which ran from East to West and divided the city into two parts. The Gran Via, that Main Street indigenous to all cities in any hemisphere (Gran Via de Colon) extended from North to South starting from the Calle de los Reyes Catolicos and outlined the boundaries from the area of the Moorish town which still remained.

The first step was the inevitable Cathedral, sixteenth century and rich in reredos and treasure, then the Capilla Real, built in florid Gothic style as the resting place of Ferdinand and Isabella. After that there was the Monastery of La Cartuja, again sixteenth century.

There was that pleasantly tired feeling that came from physical energy expended when they sat down to dinner, at a little before ten, at the Alcazaba, an elegant restaurant named after Granada's original citadel. And the knowledge that they would have another full day tomorrow, before going on to Seville, was comforting. It meant once again sleeping later in the morning, and Steve relented to the extent that he agreed they wouldn't have breakfast until ten or eleven.

"Who wants to sleep that late?" Richard asked incredulously.

"I do," Kelly said. "Oh, *do* I."

There was, unfortunately, a kind of nightclub area at the rear of the hotel, with a dais for the four piece combo and singer, and although they all went to bed at a little after midnight, the music went on until after two in the morning.

Yet it was soft Spanish music, with a sensual beat, sometimes passionate and earthy, and the singer had an exciting voice. It was not irritating, but rather hypnotic and, just as Kelly thought, *how can you sleep with that?* she was out of it.

There was no telephone call from Steve the next morning. He let her sleep. It was the birds that woke her up, and the glorious sunlight. She didn't linger in bed, as she had expected to. Life, at the moment, was too precious to be wasted. There were only a few days left. And after that, who knew what would happen?

The Alhambra, with its long avenue of clipped hedges and stately poplars, was like a dream. It was not quite the Taj Mahal, but the nearest thing to it, a kind of kissing cousin, an Elysian kingdom. Great vistas opened out from flowering courtyards and atriums; cerulean water in sunken marble pools, fountains splashing in the sun, graceful statuary and arched doorways glistened in the tender, limpid light of southern Spain.

Minarets and snake-like columns abounded, countless, sun-drenched *salas*, brilliant with tiled walls, delighted the beholder. Everything was open to the sun; there were no windows in this place, and sitting side by side with someone you thought you probably loved, you could look out, through open space, to the perfection of the gardens below and dream of a perfect life, more perfect than ordinary man ever envisioned.

This was the palace of kings.

It was probably one of the most quintessentially lovely settings in all the world. "Have you read this?" Steve asked, holding up a small red, hard-bound book.

"What is that?"

"'Tales of the Alhambra.' Washington Irving's impressions of Granada. Listen," he said, and read to her.

"Beyond the embowered regions of the Vega you behold to the south a line of arid hills, down which a long train of mules is slowly moving. It was from the summit of one of these hills that the unfortunate Boabdil cast back his last look upon Granada and gave vent to the agony of his soul. It is the spot famous in song and memory. 'The last sigh of the Moor'.

"Now raise your eyes to the snowy summit of yon pile of mountains shining like a white summer cloud in the blue sky. It is the Sierra Nevada, the pride and delight of Granada, the source of her cooling breezes and perpetual verdure and of her gushing fountains and perennial streams. It is this glorious pile of mountains that gives to Granada that combination of delights so rare in a southern city: the fresh vegetation and the temperature airs of a northern climate, with the vivifying ardor of a tropical sun and the cloudless azure of a southern sky. It is this aerial summer heat, sent down through rivulets and streams through every glen and gorge of the Alpujarras, diffusing emerald verdure and fertility throughout a chain of happy and sequestered valleys…"

He raised his head.

"Let me skip."

He began reading again.

"But enough. The sun is high above the mountains, and is pouring his full fervour upon our heads. Already the terraced roof of the tower is hot beneath our feet; let us abandon it and descend and refresh ourselves under the arcades by the Fountain of the Lions."

Steve held out his hand.

"Let us refresh ourselves," he said quietly. "Under the arcades… by the Fountain of the Lions."

CHAPTER 12

The jet left the Madrid airport at eleven fifty.

"Good-bye," Lisa Comstock said coldly to her sister-in-law, as her flight was called.

"Good-bye, Lisa, darling…"

The vulgar blonde carolled her farewells. Dolores' voice echoed through the air terminal. "Have a nice trip, darling."

She didn't turn round. She was seething. I'd like to see them both rot in hell, she thought. Dolores. And Constant. How dare they farm out her son to strangers?

How dare they!

She was not only furious, she was also frightened. That business in Rome…Constant had referred to it several times, under the guise of being solicitous.

"It must have been so humiliating for you," he'd said.

An unfit mother…would he try to pull off something like that? I must be so careful, she thought fearfully. There mustn't be anything like that again.

I have to watch myself.

She boarded the plane, and wondered if she was sick, or if it was only nerves. She felt so tired…so weak. And so terribly alone.

She should be in bed. After that bout with pneumonia in Italy. First it had been only a severe cold, and then her lungs had been infected. A week in the hospital, apathetic and her sputum examined every morning.

The scene in the hotel room, at the Excelsior, came back to her, like a crazy record playing over and over. "Room service…"

Only it hadn't been room service.

A man in her room. A few hours of love. And then the knives flashing. Revenge, Italian style…the brother of the wife of her random lover.

No, don't think about it, she told herself frantically. Don't think about that filth.

I wish I were in bed, she thought.

I wish my mother was here.

Mother. Clubwoman and philanthropist. Mother?

I hate her, she thought. I hate everyone.

Nobody would have guessed her distress. She was wonderful looking, in a good knit suit by an Italian couterier, and her hair was shining and clean and carefully tended to. Almost every woman on the flight envied her. She knew that, and she was laughing inside, laughing bitterly.

She was so *tired*.

She waved aside the light lunch, had two stiff drinks instead, and then dozed lightly. How wonderful a few minutes of forgetfulness was! She dreamed of the Chapin School, where she had prepped; she was playing volley ball in the courtyard. The cries of the other girls came to her, and when she woke it was with a reminiscent smile on her lips.

Then her mouth quivered.

But that was a lifetime ago!

Dazed, she collected her things when the plane put down, her alligator handbag, her small flight carrycase. "Have a *nice* time," the stewardess said at the exit door, with one of those sickening professional smiles.

A hell of a lot that insipid girl cared.

There was a cab almost immediately.

Others were waiting, but a driver spotted her unmistakable air of affluence.

"The Hotel Madrid," she told the driver.

"Si, *Senora*."

"And hurry, please."

"*Si.*"

She knew he would. Anyone looking at her realized she was good for a sizeable tip. It had always been that way. Money and privilege was part of her background. You paid for it; you got it.

Her face was set. She wasn't all that eager to see her son; she was only determined to drag him away from her husband's brother. The gall of the man! And that tarty wife of his…

Smoldering, she lit a cigarette. In the rear view mirror she saw the driver's curious glance. His eyes were bright and inquisitive.

She glared back at him, and his eyes slewed away.

There was a bottle—several bottles—in her bags. She was dying to get one out, take a drink. But that would have to wait. It was very hot, and the perspiration dewed her forehead and the back of her neck.

What am I and where am I going? she asked herself desolately, and leaned despondently against the leather of the seat.

"Is it much farther?"

"Very soon now," he said.

"Can't you go any faster?"

"But, *perdon*. There is a speed limit, Senora."

"All right, but as fast as you can," she said, and pulled out her cigarettes.

Why couldn't she be happy? Others were happy. Why did she have to feel so wretched?

He didn't have to die, she thought, blaming her dead husband for leaving her all alone. She had never loved him, but…he had taken care of her, kept her from—

An old, ghastly fear returned to her. It was a commonplace in these latter days. I'll end up in the gutter, she thought. I know it. I always knew it.

Why should she *think* things like that?

She saw the driver looking back at her again. This time she didn't glare. Because there was such open admiration and respect in his eyes. The man thought she was beautiful, was aristocratic.

There was veneration in his look. He could tell she was a superior person.

For a moment she felt a little better.

"Is there anything the Senora wishes?" the driver asked, fawning.

"Thank you. No. Just get me to the hotel as fast as you can. It's a very hot day."

"Very hot, yes. I will do the best I can."

All he wanted was money, she thought, her mood shifting again. A big, fat tip. Well, he'd get it. What did all that matter?

Her hands gripped the seat. That bitch, Dolores.

And Constant…

The final showdown.

"You don't deserve to have a boy like that."

"Why, why?" she had screamed. "I have a life to live! I'm a young woman. Are you any better, with that woman from the Basura…"

"My brother would turn in his grave."

I'm so tired, she thought. So God damned tired.

Her head lolled, and if she had guessed what she looked like, as she fell asleep, she would have been horrified. Her young face was suddenly haggard; her mouth fell open and her jaw dropped. The circles under her eyes became puffs, ugly and disfiguring. Her whole aspect changed, became shocking.

The driver saw the transformation, felt pity, and put his foot on the gas pedal. Poor woman, he thought vaguely. Poor American woman. They lived such crazy lives, in that insane country.

•••

The Hotel Madrid in Seville, a former monastery, was very lovely. It leaned on simplicity, was a little like the fine, quiet hotels in the

Provence of France. There was the feeling of being in a retreat, due to its monastic aspect.

An inner courtyard with great old trees was one of its most beautiful features, and before starting out on their sightseeing tour the travelers refreshed themselves there. Richard with his coke and Steve and Kelly with a *tonica*. They had arrived in Seville at just after one. The change in temperature was immediately apparent. Seville was the heart and capital of Andalusia; here the heat really scorched. You could feel it burning, thickening your tongue and slowing up speech.

Their investigatory tour of the city was faintly apathetic. Richard yawned constantly, complaining that he was terribly thirsty, and after visiting the Torre de Oro, the Tower of Gold on the banks of the Guadalquivir River, they went into a nearby *posada* and had more liquids.

"What else is there to see here?" Richard asked, his eyes half closed.

"We should go to the Plaza de Espana. Wake up, Rich."

"It's just so *hot*."

"Stop grousing."

"I'd like to take a dip in a pool."

"Sorry, the Hotel Madrid doesn't have a pool. Drink your coke and let's get going."

The Plaza de Espana was worth it, however, with its subsections celebrating, in gorgeous tiles, the medieval kingdoms and historical provinces of Spanish Iberia: Andalusia, Aragon, Asturias, Old and New Castile, Estramadura, Galicia, Leon, Murcia, Navarre and Valencia.

The sun beat down, but there were interior spaces where the sheltering stone formed cool oases, where you began to perk up… until you went outside again, and wilted in the hot glare.

Even Steve was glad to call it a day after that.

"Too muggy," he said. "Let's get back to that air conditioning."

They went to their rooms and did as the natives did; observed siesta.

At seven in the evening, it was better. There was a slight breeze stirring in the courtyard. Kelly, tanned and her nose peeling, sipped her martini, looking pensively at the tiny colored lights strung from the trees. It was still strong daylight, but the foliage darkened the garden.

The little colored lights were so pretty, so festive.

This was the last stopping-off point. In a few days she would be going home.

Steve was laughing at Richard's attempt at the Spanish "c", the lisped consonant that threw so many Americans.

"Andaluthia," he said. "It sounds as if you had a tooth missing."

Felipe, one of the men at the desk, came out and looked around, spotted them and walked over to the table.

"Buenas noches."

"Same to you," Steve said.

And then Felipe bent to him and said something in his ear.

Kelly didn't pay much attention. She was writing postcards. "I don't know," she said to Richard, when he wondered what was up. She had no sense of drama unfolding; so much for telepathy and extra sensory perception. "Dear Mother," she wrote on the back of a highly-colored postcard view of the Giralda. "Andalusia is very charming and we've all had a marvelous time. I don't know how this will end, but—"

She looked up abstractedly. How *would* it end? Was it just a summer romance?

There had been other summer romances.

Richard sucked on his coke, bottoms up. It was only an hour away from dusk, and the birds were getting ready for their night's roosting. They were chirping madly. She sipped her martini and pushed the postcards aside. How could you keep your mind on mundane things?

"I gotta have another coke," Richard said. "This heat makes me thirstier than—"

"You'll turn into a coke," Kelly said absently.

And then Steve came out from inside the darkening hotel. In his wake was a tall, stunning girl…woman. A woman with very dark hair and a too-controlled face. As if she had a stomach ache but wasn't going to let anybody know it. Her clothes were fabulous…a navy knit with a red belt. A huge alligator handbag in that expensive shade of cherry-red.

A very beautiful woman, walking just in back of Steve.

There was no way she could know, but somehow she knew.

She sat up straight. And saw Richard's open mouth, his wide, unbelieving eyes. He looked quickly at Kelly and then flushed.

"It's my mother," he said in a low voice. "Jaysus…how did she ever find me here?"

CHAPTER 13

Steve was marvelous. That was a man, Kelly thought, who knew how to handle a situation. Good or bad. Anything. He was at present ordering a third very, very dry martini for Mrs. Comstock. He had already seen to à room for her. He was all but holding her hand, and she loved it. Her eyes kept going to him.

Halfway through the third drink her voice slurred a bit. She was telling them of her misfortunes. "Imagine," she said. "I called home, to New York, and found that Richard wasn't there. Imagine!"

She turned in her chair so that she was facing Steve, with her back more or less to the others. "The child was sent over here without my knowledge or consent, and I only found out about it because I called my housekeeper."

"That must have been upsetting," Steve said soothingly.

"Everything was upsetting. There was…a little trouble… in Rome. And then I learned that my child was in Spain. With strangers!"

She had the grace to lower her eyes apologetically. "But please forgive me. You've been so…you've been better than his uncle! Imagine foisting a young boy off on perfect strangers, just like that."

She swigged a little bit more of the drink and set the glass sharply down on the table.

"I'll never forgive him. My lawyer will hear about this."

Nobody else was saying anything; except for an occasional sympathetic grunt from Steve, Mrs. Comstock was doing all the talking. Richard had his eyes down. His face was tight; he looked, suddenly, like a little old man.

I suppose I should help Steve cope, Kelly thought. But how? What could you say?

What could you say when the son looked so distressed and the mother was getting tighter by the minute? The heat, of course, made heavy drinking inadvisable, to say the least. Even Steve had been going light since they'd hit Seville. But Mrs. Comstock was packing them away, not sipping but frankly guzzling.

Her heart went out to Richard, who only a minute before had been laughing, relaxed and happy. Oh, poor child.

With the fourth drink Mrs. Comstock realized her own plight, got to her feet unsteadily but made no gaffes. She simply said, "My word, I must get some sleep. I think it would be friendly if someone would show me up to my room."

Kelly got up right away.

"I'll go with you," she said easily, and took the woman's arm.

Not that Richard's mother really needed help. She managed very well. Her eyes might be glazed and slightly watery, but she handled herself creditably. Her room was a good room, and the air conditioner hummed pleasantly.

"You're very nice," the woman said. "Now let's see…I just need my travel case. The little one, the Vuitton. A nightie, that's all. Can you find it?"

"Is this it?"

"Yes. Oh, thank you. You're so sweet. What's your name, dear?"

"Kelly Jones."

"I must remember that."

She started shedding garments. The dress, the underwear. The body underneath was rail-thin, but elegantly put together. A good, strong body…but for how long?

"That's a nice man," Mrs. Comstock murmured, pulling the nightgown over her head. "Who is he, anyway?"

"A friend of ours."

"Ours?"

"Richard's and mine."

For a second a good, sound intelligence flickered in the liquor-dazed eyes. "I see," Mrs. Comstock said dryly, and pointed to another small case. "Could I ask you to be an angel and open that?"

When opened, the case revealed a cache of liquor. There were several flasks. "That one," Mrs. Comstock said, pointing, and Kelly obediently took the flask out.

"It's vodka," the woman said, with a defiant smile. "That's always the best, you know. Maybe you don't know yet, but some day you will."

She unscrewed the cap, tipped up the flask and drank.

There was a quick little shiver of the slender shoulders in the beautiful, frothy nightgown. Then she got into bed. Her eyes, looking up from the pillows, were dark, long-lashed, unfocussed.

"I'll be all right now," she said.

"Sure there's nothing else I can get you?"

"Nothing."

"All right, then I'll…the telephone's right there, if you should need anything."

This time there was no answer.

Mrs. Comstock's eyes were closed and she was breathing regularly. The beautiful lips were parted. There was the faint sound of a snore. A very small snore, it was true, but nevertheless a snore.

There was no reason to stay longer. Richard's mother was fast asleep, gin-soaked and played out. The scent of flowers in a bowl mingled with the costly perfume of a famous designer.

It smelled nice in there, Kelly thought, closing the door.

Yet, in a certain way, it stank.

• • •

Mrs. Comstock slept all through the morning hours. Kelly was told that breakfast had been sent up, but she hadn't summoned her son to her room. Evidently she had decided that Richard was in safe hands.

Richard had, miraculously, recovered. So his mother was here, so what? She was an absentee parent, whether in spirit or in the flesh. He woke Kelly up playing castanets outside her room. When she opened the door, there he was, bright-eyed and bushy-tailed, clapping the circlets of wood together.

"Yes, Richard?"

"Steve sent me to wake you."

"Tell him I'm awake."

"When will you be down? We're waiting."

"In a very short time."

"Like what?"

"Half an hour."

"Okay. I'm drinking milk. Steve said you wanted that."

"I do. Drink a lot."

"Yes, Kelly."

"You're a good boy."

"Sometimes."

"You'll do as far as I'm concerned."

• • •

After breakfast Steve told her a few things. "You may not think I'm God's gift to women, but someone else does."

"What do you mean?"

"I had a call at four o'clock in the morning. She invited me up to her room for a drink."

"Richard's mother?"

"Uh huh."

"Oh, God."

"A lush and a nympho. Should we adopt him, do you think?"

His face was bitter. "They'll all *start* squabbling over him now. They all want him. For the wrong reasons. To butter their bread. What a family."

"Where is he now?"

"Felipe's teaching him to play the castanets."

"Oh. He was clacking them outside my room earlier."

Richard showed up a few minutes later. "Listen," he said, and raised the castanets over his head. And sure enough, he had picked up the trick.

"I'll be damned," Steve said. "He not only has brains, but manual dexterity as well."

"Oh, no, Steve," Richard said. "There *is* a trick. You just have to catch on to it and *voila*…it's as easy as rolling off a log."

"You're the smart one in the family," Steve said. "One genius is enough."

"Can I have a coke, for credits?" Richard asked, sliding into a chair.

When it came he asked what was on the agenda for the morning. "Even if she's here," he said, "we're going some place, aren't we? We always do."

Steve considered. "Look, suppose I stay here, in case she… your mother…wants something. You and Kelly can do the sights. How's that?"

"Okay, Kelly?"

"Yes, Rich. That sounds reasonable."

"You don't mind, Steve?"

"No, run along, you two. Have fun, have a ball. Okay?"

"Sure."

"Meanwhile, I'll mind the store," he said, and they went off, hand in hand, to take a gander, as Steve would have said, at the Giralda, the famous belltower of Seville which was in the center of a beautiful park where pure white pigeons, like the fabled doves of peace, strutted and spread their creamy wings.

"They're groovy," Richard breathed. "Just all white ones…oh, Kelly, aren't they super?"

He darted over to a stand, where a vendor sold cornucopias of seed. As soon as he had one of the paper cones in his hand a flock of birds flew over, perching on his shoulder, head, arms, their wings fluttering, eager for the corn.

A photographer bustled over.

"Yes, we do want pictures," Richard said eagerly. "But wait, Kelly has to be in it too."

He bought her a packet of the feed.

She posed with him, smiling uneasily; there was a pigeon right atop her head. And then the flash flared.

How odd about the birds, she thought. The dream at Cordoba and now these whirling creatures, their wings beating.

It gave her *such* a peculiar feeling.

"Ninety pesetas," the photographer said, holding out his hand. He took the money and promised to be back within the quarter hour. "Good picture, you'll see," he said boastfully.

The Giralda, towering over the city, was very Moorish, with an open balcony near its apex. "Can we go up?" Richard asked.

"Let's ask."

Yes, they could go up.

The fee was fifty pesetas; Richard insisted on paying, and they ascended, with only one or two other sightseers, to the top of the belltower.

The view was magnificent; at their feet all Seville was spread, with its glorious Tower of Gold at the edge of the blue river. There were the turrets of the Plaza de San Fernando and the Patio de Banderas.

"Look, Kelly, that's where we were yesterday," Richard said, pointing.

It was the great sweep of the Plaza de Espana at which he was looking.

"What a view," he said, sighing. "Oh, I wish I didn't have to go home."

"Everything comes to an end," she said. "We must all sooner or later realize that, Rich."

"Yeah, I guess. But all the same…"

His face was wistful.

When they went down again the pigeons circled around once more, the whirr of their wings like thunder. And now there was a man selling balloons in a corner of the park. He was crying his wares in a loud, hoarse voice.

"*Globo…globo…*"

"I want one," Richard said, and dashed over to the man with the small cart.

"*Como es?*" he demanded.

"*Ten centimos.*"

"They cost almost nothing," Richard cried, as Kelly came up to him. "Let's buy them all. Let's buy them all!"

"Richard, don't be—"

"Yes yes, I'll buy them all. I'll be the balloon man."

"Now listen, Richard…"

But he got out his wallet, quite carried away. "I want them all," he told the man, his voice quivering with excitement. "Every one of them, Senor. *Si?* How much for all of them?"

At first the man didn't understand, but then he did. He was overwhelmed at his good fortune. "*Todo?*" He started figuring frantically, using his fingers. "Two hundred pesetas, *nino, amo. No me enganas como un bobo?*"

"What's he saying?" Richard asked, flinging open his wallet.

"He wants to know if you're kidding him."

"No no. I want them all."

The man took the money, slightly dazed, and then transferred the load of balloons into Richard's arms. *"Gracias"* he cried, pocketing the cash.

"Loco…transtornado…" Laughing loudly, he wheeled his empty cart away.

"Americanos," Kelly heard him chortling happily. "Crazy *Americanos."*

A group of small children looked enviously at the little foreign boy who had bought the balloons. "You want one?" Richard asked, but of course they didn't understand. And then he was passing out the balloons.

For a few minutes the children hung back, suspicious, incredulous, not knowing what trick this was. But at last one child accepted a balloon and then a second one did.

There were sudden cries, and laughter; Richard, his fist full of balloons on sticks, was handing them out, a youthful philanthropist. It was like a carnival, it was quite beautiful, with all the shouts and the gleeful laughs and the gay colors of the balloons…red and blue and green and yellow.

"Kelly, this one is for you."

He gave her a yellow one, because she had on a yellow dress. She took the balloon and stood watching. It was a really heartwarming sight: children who couldn't communicate verbally because of the language barrier had another common language. She was so very proud of Richard, with his open heart and his sweetness and his generosity.

I love that child, she thought.

Richard was the first to release his balloon. The gas-filled globe, a bright blue, wafted up, wavered, rose, headed for the sky. Another shout went up. And then another balloon followed the first.

There was a crowd now. Adults had gathered to watch the impromptu show. Everyone was giggling, watching the children. And at last all the kids, transported, sent their balloons skyward. There were brightly colored circles of taut rubber all over the little corner of the park. Richard was laughing, was so happy. Just a little boy having a wonderful time with other laughing, screaming children.

A pang went through Kelly. If he belonged to me, she thought. To me…if he were mine…

The balloons floated through the soft air. The cries of the children shattered the quiet of the beautiful little park where the Giralda, centuries old, towered somberly. The birds, as white as snow and infected with the circus atmosphere, winged their way. One of them pierced a balloon with its beak.

Richard mingled with the crowd of frenzied children. This is beautiful, Kelly thought, almost in tears. All these happy children.

The cries mounted. For a moment she lost sight of Richard. She stood on her toes, sought for him. Then someone jostled her.

"Excuse me," she said politely.

"*Perdon.*"

"It's all right."

The man who had bumped into her was apologizing elaborately. "Please forgive me, Senora."

"It's all *right*" she said again, and started to walk away.

A balloon, helium-borne, flew in front of her face. She pushed at it and the tenuous rubber globule flew up. And then several things happened at once: a pigeon, wings whirring, flew into the air, grazing her face, and someone laughed, a child's laugh…but not Richard's.

"Richard," she called, concerned, and heard the screech of tires on asphalt. A hand grasped her elbow; she looked up, astonished, and the hand tightened.

"What do you want?" she asked, annoyed.

A face looked into hers, a quiet, dark-eyed face, a stranger's face.

It happened so quickly that she had no defenses. She was propelled by the iron grip on her arm and suddenly she was curbside. There was a big, black car there, and just as another shout of laughter went up, as a float of colored balloons was sent zooming, the door of the car was opened.

"What is this?" she started to say, dazed and confused by the noise, the laughter, the riot of color, the whirling birds and the blinding sun. "What is this?"

And then there was a sudden, excruciating pain in her ribs, at the kidney area, in the back. Her head swung round and her eyes were puzzled and then the pain weakened her and for a second she felt faint, not knowing what was happening. Everything was blurred and indistinct, and the red, red of the balloons struck her in the eyeballs.

She felt a vicious prod…and then knew that the pain was going to best her. A gust of air hit her in the forehead and suddenly she was inside the car. The car was moving. There was the sound of the pavement under the tires as the car gathered speed.

"What?" she asked numbly, and the object in her ribs was removed. She regained some of her perspective. "Richard!" she cried, and then the thing smashed down on her skull. Great circles made patterns in front of her eyes and then blackness engulfed her. Velvet darkness.

What could have happened? some reasoning part of her brain questioned, and then there was simply nothing at all.

•••

Richard, laughing, watched the balloons go up. It was better than Central Park, that was for sure. He was a paternalist at the moment; due to him, these kids were having a ball, a real groovy ball. He watched them, tolerant and enormously pleased with himself.

"Hey, this is some fun," he said, a little fatuous. "Boy, is this a ball."

The balloons bumped against each other on their way up. "Look at those crazy balloons," he cried, holding his sides to keep from dying of laughter. "Boy, what a nutty scene."

"You dig?" he asked a dark-eyed little girl near him. The inky eyes were uncomprehending. *"Bella?"* he asked. *"Broma?"*

The little face burst into a grin.

"Admirable."

Oh boy, what an afternoon. "Too bad Steve wasn't here," he said. "He would have liked this, Kelly."

He felt for her hand. But she wasn't beside him any longer. The crowd was dense. "Kelly?" he said, and pushed his way between bodies to find her.

She was here…somewhere…

"Hey, Kelly," he called, still chuckling.

She was here, somewhere. "Kelly, wasn't that something?"

He wormed his way past a group of kids and, looking for her, thought what fun they'd had.

That was her, he decided. That girl with the yellow balloon.

But it wasn't.

After a while he stopped laughing. His face took on a worried look. He started saying, "Kelly? Kelly?" and made his way through the throng.

He didn't see Kelly anywhere.

After a while he began pushing, quite rudely, using his elbows. "Hey, Kelly," he said, over and over again. But her answering voice failed to reach him.

Where the hell *was* she?

The crowd began to disperse. The carnival was over. All the balloons were gone now. And still no sign of Kelly's dark head, her tall, lissome figure.

She had to be here…somewhere.

Soon the little island in the park, which only a short time before had been so gala, was almost deserted. Passersby came and went.

Kelly wasn't anywhere. She wasn't *anywhere*.

He felt his face crumpling. He didn't like that. But after all he was only a ten year old kid, and his friend…why, she wasn't here. She wasn't *here*.

A middle-aged woman saw him standing there, looking round uncertainly. She said something to him, but of course he couldn't understand; she spoke in Spanish. Yet he clutched her arm.

"I'm looking for my friend," he said in a small voice.

"Perdon?"

And then, shamefully, the tears came. Because he didn't know what it was, but he did know that something terrible had happened to Kelly. He *knew* it. "Hotel Madrid," he said at last, as the woman patiently questioned him. "Hotel Madrid, *el favor…*"

She got him back to the hotel and he thanked her. He wasn't crying any more; he was beyond that. He was terrified. Not knowing why, but terrified. He tried to pay the woman for the taxi, digging out his wallet. But she made him put it away and took him to the desk clerk.

"Felipe, Kelly's gone," Richard said tremulously. "We were in the park, near the Giralda and then she wasn't there any more."

There was a long confab between the desk clerk and Richard's rescuer and then suddenly Steve was there. Richard clung to him.

"I can't find Kelly, Steve."

"What do you mean, can't *find* her?"

"I can't," he said piteously. "I gave her a balloon, a yellow one, and everyone was laughing. And then there were only a few people left there, and Kelly wasn't—"

He said passionately, "She wouldn't leave me just like that. You know that, Steve."

The man looked at Felipe, at the woman who had brought Richard home, and then sat Richard down.

"Okay, cool it," he said. "Sit. Now. Tell me about it. What happened?"

"We went up to the top of the tower. The Giralda. Then when we came down there was a man with balloons. I bought them all. I gave one to Kelly, a yellow one. Then I gave the rest to all the kids who were there. We let them go up. It was…"

"Yes. Take it easy, Rich."

"And then when it was all over, Kelly wasn't there. Steve, she was gone. This lady brought me home."

And then he was crying again. He was sick about it, but he couldn't help it. "Because where could she be?" he asked brokenly. "How can someone just disappear like that?"

"It's okay."

Steve straightened up. "What do you think?" he asked Felipe.

"I don't know." The clerk looked worried. "I don't know what to think, Senor."

Richard watched Steve become as helpless as he himself felt. The man, the big, strong man, looked dazed. As if he didn't know what the hell to do next. It was the child's first experience with adults who were totally ineffectual. Some of his faith, some of his feeling that grown people were godheads, was lost at that moment. But he gained something else. The knowledge that being no longer a child was the key to wisdom and strength.

It was then that his tears stopped.

Tears, he saw, weren't going to help. He got up off the chair and stuck his hands in his pockets. "What are we going to do, Steve?" he asked.

The man looked down at him. "Let me think," Steve said. "Just let me think. The thing is, I can't seem to—"

His face tightened. "If anything's happened to Kelly, I'll—"

"But what could happen in Seville?" Felipe asked wonderingly. "This is a quiet city."

The woman who had brought Richard home finally went off. Quite clearly, she didn't want anything; she had only been sorry for the little boy. But Steve insisted on paying the cab fare, and he added a substantial amount to it.

"And I'll remember your kindness always," he said.

After she'd left he pumped Richard again.

"Tell me from the beginning," he said.

"I…we…we went up to the belltower. The Giralda. It was a nice view and then we came down again. After that there was the man with the balloons. I wanted all of them and he said it would be two hundred pesetas. He seemed glad to sell them all. And then I gave all the kids a balloon."

"Yes?"

"Kelly, too. I gave her a yellow one. Because she was wearing a yellow dress."

"Yes, and then?"

"Then I let my balloon go. After a while, the other kids did the same thing. The balloons were all going up into the air."

"Where was Kelly all this time?"

"Standing there. I *thought*. I mean…why *shouldn't* she be there? Where would she *go?*"

"And then?"

"And then the crowd thinned out. The balloons were gone, and the children went too. There was hardly anybody left."

"And no sign of Kelly?"

"No! She just wasn't there!"

"We must call the police," Felipe said excitedly.

"Wait, let me think."

"But Senor—"

"Just let me be for a minute or two." Steve's face was pale under his tan. "I have to think, damn it."

"*Si*, Senor, but even in Seville…"

"Shove it," Steve said savagely. "Let me think, for Christ's sake."

Richard stood there, stunned. Kelly had been there one minute, holding her balloon, a canary yellow, a smile on her face. And then, in the next moment, she had been gone.

He bit his lip. It wouldn't do any good to bawl. That wouldn't help Kelly.

But who would want to hurt her?

"Please, Steve," he said. "Can't you think of something?"

CHAPTER 14

First of all she was conscious of sweat drenching her. Coming to, slowly and painfully, she felt the moisture on her forehead, between her breasts; the hair on the back of her neck was plastered down.

It was so hot.

Then the pain came creeping back.

Piecemeal, she remembered. The hard object in her ribs…and then the whack on the side of her head. The movement of the strange car…

She came to all at once and, as she lifted her head, agony shot through her and once more she went under.

The next conscious moment was when the movement of the car stopped. Suddenly there was utter quiet; the throbbing of the motor ceased, and she opened her eyes to hear the twitter of a bird. Next, there was a faint rustling of leaves and after that, a voice saying, "Let's get her inside, Pablo."

There was country quiet; she was being lifted out through the car door, in a man's arms. A huge tree, its leafy branches trembling in a sprightly gust, was a green blot; she saw the blue of the sky, some powdery clouds, and heard the bird sing again.

"Where am I?" she asked, through dry lips.

"Shall I hit her again?" she heard someone say in Spanish. She drew into herself, waiting for the blow. Please, she thought. Not again…

"No perdio el control…"

No blow came. How grateful she was for that, and for the stern adjuration of the second man to his friend. "Don't lose your cool," was what he had substantially said.

Everything was taken in stride. Why? It didn't matter. What was happening didn't matter…for the moment. She simply didn't want to be hurt again. She would be good. Just as long as they didn't hurt her.

"Can you walk?" a voice asked, in English.

"I'll try," she said.

She was set down on her feet. Unsteadily, she stood and shook, but yes, she could walk. "So, good," the good voice said, and a hand went under both of her arms, as if she were recovering from an operation and a nurse was helping her down the corridor. She believed that for a moment. So she had undergone surgery. And now was ambulatory...

She put one foot in front of the other, like a good girl, and heard the bad voice say, "Kick her in the ribs; give her something to remember you by."

It wasn't a hospital. Reality flooded back. And fear with it.

Who were these people? What had happened?

Richard!

The balloons, the white doves, the—

And now her faculties began to gather together. She peered around. "Richard," she said. "Where's Richard?"

"Shut up," the good voice said quietly.

The steps, four of them, were difficult to negotiate. "All right, one more," the good voice said, urging her on. "That's it."

The cool, dark interior of wherever they were helped. She wanted to dry the back of her neck with her hand, but someone slapped it away.

"Quiet, now, and you won't be hurt."

"Please...where is this?"

"Sit down and shut up."

She was lowered into a chair. She sat there obediently, the headache claiming almost all of her attention. It hurts so much, she thought gravely.

"Could I have an aspirin?" she asked.

How thick her voice sounded. How craven. How unlike her...

Was this the end of the line?

An inner voice asked the question. The turbulence of her thoughts was due to pain, shock and the sheer surprise of the attack on the…street corner…with the balloons…the crowds…the childish laughter…

She couldn't *think*.

Couldn't think straight.

The perspiration poured down her neck, forehead, upper lip. Her dress stuck to her. She couldn't seem to sit straight, either; the man was almost holding her up. His touch was not ungentle, but she was conscious of the dark gaze from someone else…the other man, the one with the bad voice. Her eyes saw what he was like. Swarthy, disgusting, sweaty and like an animal in a zoo.

That man had wanted to hit her again.

She shuddered, feeling the bile coming up into her throat. The pain lessened as the nausea grew. She swallowed past the lump in her throat, felt faint again, and started to slide down in the chair.

"Jola…"

The man holding her up put both arms around her. She smelled his rank odor, gagged. I'm going out again, she thought, and then heard another voice. Blinking, she recognized it.

"Ah, so," the other voice said, and she knew someone else had come into the room.

Her eyes opened again; amazement stunned her. If she had been almost out of it a second before, the surprise of the familiar voice brought her back to consciousness. It was a croupy, emphysematic voice, the familiar voice of Senor Nascimento.

"So, very good," he said, and then, after a sudden, shocking silence, there was a sharp expletive.

"Merdia…"

She waited, looking up with blurred eyes into the gaunt face of the man on the plane. His expression was unbelieving. Their glances locked.

"*Por Dios…*" he said, almost hissing it.

There was another brief silence and then an explosion. "But this is not the mother!" Senor Nascimento cried. "What is this that you have done?"

The mother? What did that mean…

Suddenly the South American started screeching. "Stupid! The wrong woman…stupid…*infructuoso imbecile…loco…malo…*"

Dimly, it started to make sense. The wrong woman. *This is not the mother.*

Why, it was Richard's mother these people had meant to kidnap. Richard's pathetic mother.

There was a garble of excited Spanish. Raised voices. Screams, imprecations. "Stupid, stupid," Senor Nascimento kept shrieking. "Now what to do, you *louse.*"

She sat there patiently, and she knew. These men had made a mistake. It was supposed to have been Lisa Comstock but instead they had snatched her.

And now what?

Now, well, what else? She would have to be silenced. Cold, craven terror surged through her. She would never be allowed to leave this place alive. My head, she thought, but it was compensation. Her head didn't hurt as badly as all that, but it was a substitute for cowardly, sick fear. They'll kill me. Just to shut me up. They'll kill me and bury me in a ditch somewhere.

The voices faded away, and she still sat there, numbed. The light, filtering through a slatted blind, hurt her eyes. She put a hand over them and then, like a rag doll, slid down in the chair. Another hand went out to ward off the floor that was coming up at her, and she felt the soft pile of carpet between her fingers.

Laughing helplessly, with tears seeping through the laughter, her head came to rest on the cool tile between the scatter rugs.

This can't be real, she thought.

She must be dreaming.

There were thirty-odd hospitals in Madrid and the outlying districts and Steve called them all. The answer was always the same.

"No, Senor. There is no one by that name here."

"She might be. I have to point out that she might not know anything. It's possible she could be a victim of amnesia."

But it was no good. No amnesiac, epileptic, heart patient, traffic victim or autistic personality had been logged in in the past twenty-four hours.

"The police," Felipe kept insisting.

"Not yet."

"But why, Senor?"

"Because," Steve sat down and put a hand over his eyes, "I'm not sure. But I'm afraid to bring them in on this thing."

"For what reason?" The desk clerk was incredulous.

"I'm not sure," Steve said wretchedly. "But believe me, Felipe, I have my reasons, even though I'm not too clear about them myself."

"Something must be done," the clerk said, wringing his hands. "That beautiful girl…"

"Just give me a little while longer."

It was about seven in the morning when the call came through from Madrid.

It was a woman's voice, sounding very far away, on a poor connection with a feedback.

"Senor Connaught?"

Steve pressed the receiver to his ear. "Yes, who's this?"

"This is Joia." The old woman's voice was raspy. "You're there, Senor?"

"Yes, Joia. What is it?"

"Senora Comstock…they have taken her, *si?* I can tell you where."

"Senora Comstock?" He took the receiver away from his ear, looked at it in astonishment and then put it back. "What are you talking about, Joia? There's nothing wrong with Richard's mother. Kelly's gone. I can't seem to trace her whereabouts. It's Kelly. What are you trying to say?"

There was the sound of an *indrawn* breath. Then, "The Senorita? I don't understand…"

"Kelly's disappeared," Steve said rapidly. "What is all this about Senora—"

There was an abrupt silence, as if she had gone away. Then a weird, choked sound, a gasp, and the phone went dead.

"Joia," Steve said, then said it again. "Joia? Are you there?"

But he knew she wasn't. You could tell when there was a blank line.

He had been cut off.

He called operator.

"I was talking to Madrid," he said. "My line was disconnected."

"I'm sorry, sir." The correct voice was formal. "Please give me the number you called, sir."

"I didn't call them, they called me. It's Paseo de la Castellana, Madrid. Can you get them for me, please. It's urgent."

"Yes, sir. Please stand by."

She rang back a few minutes later. "I am sorry, sir, but there is no answer when I ring the Madrid number."

"But there has to be," he shouted. "There are about a dozen servants, and…there has to be! Keep trying."

"Yes, sir."

"Now what?" Richard asked, wearing down his fingernails.

"The American consul, that's the only thing I can think of. Christ, how can someone disappear just like that?"

"It was my fault," Richard said miserably. "I should have taken better care of her."

Steve brushed his hand across the child's head. "You stupid kid. It wasn't your fault," he said harshly. "Stop scarifying yourself. If it was anybody's fault it was mine. There was something screwy all along. I should have realized it."

CHAPTER 15

The soft green of trees, the broad sweep of grass…it was so lovely, so lovely. There was the stern fortress, its crenellated walls rising high, formidable, impregnable. But outside the forbidding walls sunlight swept across the moat and the foliaged compound outside. There were soft clouds in the sky.

Kelly was lying on the grass, quiet, happy, with the fortress walls behind her. It was long ago, she thought. Way, way back people had been incarcerated and tortured in those deep, dark dungeons of the castle. Avila, in the twentieth century, was liberated. There were no more racks, no wheels, no Iron Maidens. Just the same she was glad she was outside the fortress, on the green grass at its foot.

She was glad to be free.

She was looking, with eyes still badly focussed, at an etching of the Palacio de Avila. It was on the south side of the wall, beside her brass bed, and what seemed at first to be a realistic scene was only a picture on the wall.

Solemnly, she stared at the picture, came back to earth.

I'm a prisoner, she thought.

She raised herself. Instantly, the thread of pain that shot through her mounted, sent her reeling back again. They hit me with something hard, she thought, almost laughing with the insanity of it. They had hit her, knocked her out and then…

And then Senor Nascimento had said they'd taken the wrong woman.

They hadn't wanted her. But they'd taken her. And now they'd never let her go…that was, not alive.

She leaned on an elbow. Standing peacefully in a small, lovely park, watching the balloons rise into the sky. Such a lovely day… and the children laughing…

Richard laughing…

Oh, my God, she thought. I can't believe this! That I'm here…

She sprang up, falling instantly, weak and uncoordinated, sprawling on the floor.

How could such a thing be, she asked herself, and was immobilized with fear, dread and frustration. I can't stand being here, she thought, hysterical. Why should this happen to me?

Painfully, she got to her feet, stood, wobbly, holding on to the edge of the bed. I can't believe it, she thought somberly. That this hideous thing should happen to me.

The door was firmly closed.

She hobbled over and tried it. It didn't do any good. It was bolted from the outside.

Wanting to pound on it, she knew better. She didn't want another blow on the head. She walked unsteadily over to the window. It wasn't barred. But it was so far above the courtyard level that, were she to jump, she would surely break a leg, an arm, or very possibly her neck.

She turned away and circled the room, feeling out the boundaries of her prison. There was only the brass bed, a low chest of drawers, an armoire. And then she saw the other door that led into a small bathroom. Inside was a toilet and a sink.

There was no medicine chest, no mirror.

She used the toilet, found a cracked, dry bar of soap in a niche, dried her hands with tissue from her handbag. And then walked around the room again, looking for something that could be a weapon.

But there was nothing. Absolutely nothing.

She sat on the edge of the bed, blank-eyed. Her fate was sealed. There had been a mistake, a ridiculous mistake, but they would now have to cover up. They would never let her go.

She fantasied. In a ditch, covered over with leaves. Bloodied, dead, left to the changing seasons, until her remains were only bones. She would lie, in some gully, for years upon years. She would rot there.

Desperate, uncomprehending, she looked up at the picture of the Avila fortress, at the green grass and the beautiful leafy trees, the wide open spaces outside the grim fortress. And then stood up, an idea forming in her mind. She went to the picture, felt it, dragged it off its hook. It was about seventeen by twenty inches, and it was heavy, heavy…

The picture was a weapon. This could kill someone…if you hit him at the base of the skull.

She hefted it, feeling its weight. If you were to catch someone unaware, bring it down with all your might, you could incapacitate your victim.

The idea jelled in her mind.

What else was there? This, at least, was a kind of defense. There was nothing else she could think of.

And then she recoiled from the thought. To break a person's skull.

And if she tried, and failed, they'd hurt her. They could do terrible things to her.

This was what solitary confinement could do to a person. Turn them into a coward, into a quivering mass of jelly. I won't be like that, she thought, gritting her teeth. I won't fall to pieces. I *won't*.

She went over and took the picture off the wall again.

It was very heavy and yes, it was a perfect weapon.

She hung it up again.

And at last, exhausted, got into bed again.

Eyes blurred, looking up at the picture of the Avila fortress, she longed for the green grass and the beautiful, leafy trees, the wide open spaces outside the grim fortress.

Let me be free, she thought, winding her arms around herself. Please, God, let me be free.

• • •

Darkness.

Waking, instantly apprehensive, Kelly tensed. There was a sound.

She lay there, cringing.

A scrape of the key in the lock. The door opened. A beam of light met her blind eyes. Then there was a lamp flicked on in the room.

It hurt her eyes, and she shaded them. Only it wasn't a lamp, it was a flashlight.

Someone came into the room.

"Senorita?" It was the good voice.

"Yes," she said carefully.

"Your supper. Eat."

He came over to the bed with a tray. "Your supper," he said, and set a tray down on the floor.

She didn't say anything, and he went on. "Good food. Rice. Lobster and beef. Please. Eat."

He went to the door again.

Framed there, he said, "Is there anything you want?"

"Oh, yes. Aspirin. My head hurts."

"Very good. In a few minutes."

He went out again. The door closed behind him.

She looked at the contents of the tray. The man had left the flashlight on the floor. It was the only light. The food smelled tantalizing. How could you have an appetite when you were in such a ghastly situation?

I won't eat it, she thought. It was probably poisoned. She wouldn't touch it with a ten foot pole.

She turned away, resolute.

In a few seconds, aroused by the aroma of the dinner on the floor, she swung her legs over the bed and looked at it. What did it matter if it was poisoned? That would be better than having one's throat cut.

It was delicious. She ate every morsel. After a while the door opened again and the man came in.

He looked at the empty plate, and then held out his hand. There were four tablets; she took them.

"Aspirin," he said.

He waited while she put them in her mouth and then washed them down with the glass of red wine she hadn't touched. She said thank you, and he bowed, picked up the tray. He went out and took the flashlight with him. He murmured something, which might have been "Good night," but she wasn't sure. The door closed, with a firm thud, and a bolt was drawn. She was alone again, in the darkness. She got up after a while, felt every inch of the wall for a light switch, but found nothing.

She sat quietly on the edge of the bed for a long time, until she couldn't bear her thoughts any longer. The aspirin had calmed her and, in spite of everything, she slept. It was an excessively warm night, but she pulled the covers over her, nesting inside them. She was, of course, exhausted. Even fright had left her. There was only a deep sopor.

There was something so wonderful about sinking into forgetfulness. All thoughts left her, and she lay, supine, a part of the black night.

• • •

It was just past nine when Steve called Lisa Comstock's room.

Her voice was blurred and thick.

"Yes?"

"This is Steve Connaught."

"*Who?*"

"Please," he said. "Wake up, would you mind? The girl's not back yet."

"Oh."

"I have to talk to you."

"Yes." She really did sound concerned. "I'm so sorry." There was a short silence and then she said, "Oh, yes, just let me get myself together. Could you wait…about an hour, that's all. My God, how terrible. What could have happened?"

"I don't know, maybe you can shed some light," he said.

"Oh, I hope so. Is Richard all right?"

"Richard's fine."

"What time is it?"

"A little after nine."

"In the morning?"

"Yes, Mrs. Comstock. In the morning. A.M."

She groaned.

"Mrs. Comstock, you will come down?" he said, gritting his teeth. "You must realize how important it is."

"Oh, yes. I'll be right down. Just as soon as I can."

"Please hurry. I'll be waiting for you in the lounge."

"Yes." She was obedient. "I'll get right up. I promise."

* * *

"Tell me what happened," Steve said to Lisa. "From the time you got to Madrid."

"Well. I had a flight from Rome. Then I got a taxi to Constant's house. He was horrid. He hates me. I hate him too. He's an opportunist, I always told Lawrence that."

"So you left the airport and went to the Villa Bondadoso. You had a talk with your brother-in-law?"

"He was *so* irritating."

"You were upset about Richard."

"Wouldn't you be?"

"I guess so. You stayed there overnight?"

"Yes, but I couldn't sleep. So I called the airport and booked a flight here."

She put a hand to her throat. "I'm dry," she said. "Order me a drink, will you? Vodka on the rocks."

He called the waiter over.

"That's better," she said, when the drink came. "Thank you." She was almost humble. "You seem to be a decent man. You understand about these things, don't you?"

Yes, he understood about a lot of things. Who was he to cast the first stone? He was gentle. But he had to pick her brain. "You booked your flight, what then?"

"Uh…the flight was for six o'clock in the evening."

She fished in her handbag for cigarettes. Kelly had nice things, good clothes and all the rest of it. But women like this, like Richard's mother and Dolores Comstock, had alligator bags that ran into the hundreds of dollars. Pucci stuff, Gucci stuff. They were bitches, really, while Kelly worked hard.

Anger surged through him.

He fished for his lighter and just then she brought forth some matches from her handbag. He picked them up and lit her cigarette.

The matchbook lay on the table between them. She started talking again, but he wasn't listening. He was looking at the matchbook. At first it didn't mean all that much, but his subconscious absorbed it and then it meant a great deal.

"Where did you get this?" he asked Lisa.

"Get what?"

"These matches."

"I don't know. How should I know?"

"You have to remember. It's important. Where did you get them?"

"For God's sake, with all that's happened, I'm supposed to remember where I got some *matches?*"

She was very nearly hysterical. She picked up the book of matches and hurled it to the floor. "So much for your God damned questions," she cried. "Are you crazy?"

Steve bent down and picked up the matchbook. The name on the cover was Hotel Indepencia, Madrid, Spain.

Where he and Kelly had gone to hunt up the Nascimentos, who had checked out a couple hours earlier.

"You took a cab from the Madrid airport?"

"Yes."

"Then you stayed overnight at the Villa Bondadosa."

"Yes."

"And then decided to come to Seville."

"Yes!"

"Who drove you to the airport in Madrid? Did you take a cab?"

"I was driven."

"By whom?"

"The family."

"Constant?"

"No. Dolores."

"She was at the wheel of the car?"

"Certainly not. The chauffeur was at the wheel. Jose."

"I see," he said, his brain whirling. So that was the way it had been.

"What does it matter?"

"There were just the three of you? Dolores, Jose and you?"

"Yes, but what are you trying to—"

"Did you smoke in the car?"

"I don't know! I always smoke. Of course I—"

"Do you have a lighter?"

"I did. It was stolen. Pure gold. Someone stole it. What does it matter?"

"So you needed matches to light your cigarette."

"So what?"

"Who lit your cigarette?"

"Who? The chauffeur, of course. Who else, Santa Claus?"

"So the chauffeur provided the matches."

"No, Jesus Christ did," she said profanely, and her face was ugly, ugly.

"You needed a light and the chauffeur slowed the car and passed back the matches. Is that right?"

"Naturally! What was he supposed to do, rub sticks together?"

She followed his eyes, looking at the matchbook with its gilt lettering, Hotel Indepencia. And a shred of intelligence, of honest concern, lit her eyes.

"Do these mean anything?" she asked.

They meant everything, Steve thought, staring at the matchbook. The Hotel Indepencia, where he and Kelly had gone to talk to the Nascimentos, who had checked out with no forwarding address. That meant that there was a tie-in between the South American couple and the Comstock family in Madrid. That meant—

"What is it, what is it?" the woman was asking. "Tell me, for God's sake. What are you *thinking?*"

He looked up.

"Why, your relatives want to get Richard away from you," he said. "It's as simple as that. They want it so badly that they arranged for your sudden demise. I know who they're working with. This matchbook tells me that. Only they mistook Kelly for Richard's mother, for you."

The woman's face paled. "You're not talking sense."

"Yes I am. I'm talking sense. And now there's only one thing left to do. Put it squarely in the lap of the American Consul."

His face worked.

"And hope for the best," he said, out of a tight throat. "I can't put it off any longer. Maybe I've waited too long as it is."

CHAPTER 16

A dream about green grass, and the smells thereof, and the gentle swish of leaves in the trees. Cool, fresh air, the sounds of animal life…

It was, of course, the sound that brought her out of sleep.

A stealthy sound, a key turning in the lock.

Her body gathered itself together in the blackness.

The lock turned and there was the sound of someone sliding into the room. It was not the good man. The good man hadn't come in so furtively. This was different, was terribly different.

So tense that the calves of her taut legs hurt, she slid out from under the covers. Thank God, now, for the darkness. She was as quiet as a mouse. She had to be so terribly quiet. Because…

Because she knew it, sensed it. This was the bad man.

Trembling, she tiptoed round to where the picture was on the wall.

Now, she thought. It was her only chance. Now.

There was the gust of a wine-soaked breath.

Her eyes were accustoming themselves to the dark. But his weren't. She had a very slight advantage. She heard him groping his way to the bed. Heard his hard breathing. Knew, at once, his intention. So then, it *was* the pig, the sadist. She was slated for death, but before that this animal was determined to use her body.

She stopped shivering. Now she knew that she wanted to kill. She wasn't afraid any longer; she was filled with hate. She would do it.

Standing there, scarcely breathing, she waited. And heard him go down on the bed. Hard, vicious, brutal…only a disgusting animal.

In less than five seconds he knew she wasn't there. She heard his oath.

Now, she thought. It had to be now.

She reached up, freed the picture from the wall. It was heavy… that was good, but her hands had started trembling again. She had to do this. She *had* to.

His curses rang out. He was no longer quiet. A vicious barrage of Spanish was unleashed, and he stumbled about; in the dim light she saw his flailing arms. She felt when he neared her; smelled it, too. The disgusting breath was on her cheek. And then fingers touched her. Her flesh crawled and suddenly she was totally calm, totally prepared. He grasped her arm, gloating and with a loud cry of triumph. The sweaty hand slid up her arm, to the shoulder, and then she raised the heavy picture and brought it down on his head.

The metal frame hit against bone.

The sound was horrendous, bringing water into her mouth.

There was a thick cry of agony, and then a ghastly groan. The hand on her arm slid away, like soft bananas, rotten and decayed. It was so hard for her not to scream, not to give way to frayed nerves. But she was silent. The heavy body hit the floor. And the place where the picture frame had smashed down on him was wet…slimy, hot, slippery. Her hands touched the wet place; she smelled the hot, new letting of blood, retched, turned away, circled the inert body and placed, with utmost precision and caution, the picture on top of the bed. Then she moved slowly and silently to the door.

It was open.

Scarcely believing it, pausing fearfully for one paralyzed moment, she stepped out into the hall.

There was utter quiet.

It couldn't be this easy, she thought. Someone would come and hit her again.

It couldn't possibly be this simple.

But it was.

The house was dark. She maneuvered the stairs and got to the bottom. In the pale light from outdoors she saw the door, went to it, saw a bolt, prayed, and slid it back.

It made scarcely a sound.

And then she was outside.

She didn't have time to think. She simply walked, her muscles taut and controlled, through the courtyard to the open road beyond. She walked quietly and purposefully for about a quarter of a mile. And then started running. A shoe came off; she found it and slipped into it again. And ran on. It was a main highway, but there were no cars. It was the middle of the night. There was nothing, only the empty road and the dark night. She was glad for the darkness, praying only that there would be no blinding headlights suddenly, no big, black car zooming up behind her.

Blisters formed on her heels. But she scarcely felt them.

It was impossible to know how long she had been walking. There was still no sign of light in the sky. Her watch had stopped: she hadn't thought to wind it. It could be midnight, or it could be, four in the morning.

She had no idea where she was headed.

She sat down finally. She was out of breath and she had the feeling that she was all alone on planet earth. She was the last living person in the world. Loneliness was a killing thing.

There must, sooner or later, be a house somewhere.

She got up again and trudged on, her feet sore and swollen. The road turned, a low-lying branch brushed against her cheek, moist with dew and cobwebbed.

Ugh. And then, rounding the bend, she saw the lighted towers in the distance, thought first that it was a mirage, and then knew what lay ahead, just over the hill.

An airport.

The conning towers, winking their lights, rise high.

The Sevilla Airoporto.

It was, it was!

The airport.

She was home.

"For you," the night desk clerk said to Steve, who was sitting in the lobby, waiting for morning.

He sprang up.

"Yes?" He spoke into the phone.

"Mr. Connaught?"

"Yes, yes. This is he."

"Someone to speak to you. Please hold on."

An interminably long silence and then a golden voice, a beautiful, beloved voice.

"Steve? It's Kelly."

"Jesus Christ, it's about time," he said, putting a hand to his mouth. "Where the hell are you?"

"At the airport. San Pablo. Could you come and get me?"

"Are you all right, Kelly?"

She might have been playing bridge with friends. Her voice was as cool as glass.

"Sure. I'm fine. But will you come?"

"I don't know how long it takes to get there," he said. "But if you budge I'll break every bone in your body. Just sit. I'll be there."

"I won't move," she said, and laughed.

"Good-bye," he said. "And I love you."

...

It was daylight when they started back to the Hotel Madrid. The sky was pink and violet and the sun was beginning to shine through clouds.

"Gee, I'm sorry, Steve," Kelly apologized once or twice, as she fell over, dozing, against his shoulder. "Am I interfering with your driving?"

"You're interfering with my breathing," he said. "But then you did from the beginning. You smell like a rose, and I always did go for roses."

"I sweat like a pig," she said. "It was so hot in that house. I'm sure I'm rancid. How can you stand it?"

"Put your little feet up," he said tenderly. "Just be comfortable. You're sure they didn't hurt you?"

"No. But I may have killed someone."

"I hope you did," he said harshly. "I hope he suffered, the way I…and you…"

But he was talking to the air. She was fast asleep. He gunned the motor. This sweet kid has to get to bed, he thought.

CHAPTER 17

Madrid, June fourteenth, 1970.

Richard wrote the date on Hotel Ritz stationery. He and his mother were staying there, instead of at Uncle Constant's, before returning to the States.

He nibbled the top of the pen and then addressed his letter.

"Dear Aunt Elizabeth."

He put the pen down. What a wonderful time they'd had, he and Steve and Kelly. What a glorious time.

Why couldn't things always be like that?

He took the pen again and started writing.

"Incredible things have happened in the last week or so. I'm sure you've had some word sent to you, about everything. Of course I suspected Uncle Constant, but it was Dolores and the chauffeur. You see, Dolores thought that, with Mummy out of the way, she and Uncle Constant could have me, since I seem to be worth a great deal of money, through Grandma's trust fund. Kelly, my friend, was kidnaped, and almost lost her life, but in the end justice triumphed.

"I feel sorry for Mummy, but she has problems I don't understand. I wish, you know, that I could live with you. I don't know whether you would like that, but—"

He read over what he had written, and then tore the paper into little pieces and sat there, despondent.

It will never be like that, he thought. I have a mother, and I have to live with her.

•••

Constant Comstock was in his library. He had just returned from a two hour session with the American Counsul in Madrid. He had cleared himself of a heinous charge, but it was, nevertheless, a black mark against him. In all his years as a career diplomat there had never been the slightest suggestion of wrong-doing.

Now, at this late date, there was.

His own wife had negotiated with a shady South American couple—not even Spanish—for a kidnaping and death. The very name was an insult…Nascimento, meaning "birth."

Death-dealers…with a name like that.

And Dolores, in the most devious way, had rifled his files, found the information on the subject pair and used it to her advantage.

Truly, women were vile creatures.

Vile and filthy.

Three persons were now under surveillance. Lucia and Jorge Nascimento. And Jose Chavez. They would be caught in the net, all three of them.

These facts were all neatly arranged in a manila folder labeled COMSTOCK, CONSTANT.

They had dirtied his name. His good name.

My brother was lucky, he thought. My brother died.

He was alone to handle this…this ugly, dirty thing.

So this was what his life had come to. A life once so filled with promise.

In the end, everyone was a loser. What had been was taken away. The road led downhill, irrevocably, and the final victor was death. Life was a cheat, a fraud. It was a losing proposition.

• • •

"What do you want?" Dolores asked uneasily, when her husband said he had some business with her. He had cornered her in her bedroom.

"You did it for me, you'll tell me," he said. "Oh yes, you're beautiful. You look like a Madonna."

She screamed. The whip lashed out, catching the gold of the sun. It hissed, but it didn't touch her. Curling, smoking, it burned on the tiled floor.

"No," Dolores cried, the blood rushing to her head. She had never before known fear like this fear.

An arm was raised again.

She gasped, put her hands up.

"Constant! For God's sake! Yes, I did it for you."

This time the whip didn't hit the floor. It curled across the woman's tanned, splendid shoulders, wound itself in a terrible caress, laid open an arc of tender flesh.

The scream came again. Foam bubbled at the corners of the woman's mouth. The blood surged to the surface across her collar bones.

The next scream was cut off in mid-air as the whip swung once more. This time she fell to the floor. She smelled her own blood, was blinded with pain and desperation. With the third blow she was speechless, able only to mew like a cat, her almost blind eyes watching the swing of the whip.

And then that was about all. The fourth lash swept across her face, her beautiful face. Sinking, soaked in blood and drowning in white agony, she knew that her beauty was gone forever. Even the physical punishment couldn't equal that hideous knowledge. But it was all soon forgotten. Her eyes closed, her senses failed, and Constant Comstock, watching her pitilessly, threw away the whip and went down and got into the car.

He drove steadily, in control of himself, and thought, I have loved this city, and remembered its topography, its history, its legends. It kept him company, the lore and splendor of his adopted Madrid, as he drove to the pine-clad mountains of the Guadarrama, climbing steadily, and the breezes were fragrant with the scent of pine and broom.

Near the top he turned the car, idled the motor as he looked down at the valleys below. Just before he put the car in motion again he looked up at those clear, blue Velazquez skies.

Then he took a deep breath, gunned the motor, and let her go. The turns were serpentine. For a few minutes his hands guided the wheel, then he sat on them. The car, on its own power, zoomed down, gaining speed. There was an overwhelming impulse to put his hands back on the wheel, but Constant Comstock closed his eyes and, perhaps praying, kept his palms down, letting the vehicle go where it would. It has to be, he reasoned with himself. There was no other way.

He heard the rending crash as the car hit an impediment in the road. His eyes flew open and his hands came up from the seat. But they didn't go to the wheel. He saw the precipice below, felt the car careening toward it, and his hands went to his face, blotting out what was going to happen next.

He was Daedelus, winged, flying into the blue...

The impetus, as the car hurtled the cliff, smashed him against the roof of the tonneau: as the impact knocked him senseless there was one last thought.

And yet I did love her...

After a dozen overspins the car came to rest on a lower plateau. It caught fire almost at once. Plumes of red soared into the sky. And after a while there was only the smoldering. There were several annual accidents in the dangerous Guadarrama mountains. This time it was no accident, but would be lumped with the rest of the fatal disasters that, yearly, took place in the mountain passages where once a girl named Carmen had taken refuge with her lover, Don Jose.

CHAPTER 18

Lisbon.

The hotel was the Tivoli, on the Avenida da Liberdade, a broad, gorgeous thoroughfare rising from the sea in a steep incline and culminating at its top in the Praco de Marques de Pombal, where a gigantic statue of the grandee towered at its center, its gaze fixed on the River Tagus down below.

They spent most of the day at the Estoril. It was easier to hire a car and driver, so they did that. They sat and drank and then rented bathing suits and swam in the blue water, lay on the white sand and slept, holding hands.

The day passed all too soon. Later, back at the hotel, they had an early dinner and then went to bed.

Kelly packed, soberly, was ready the following morning. From time and training she was in Ops at the airport at the proper time. "There's a California film star in first class," she was told. "Confidentially," the briefing instructor added, "he's a notorious drunk."

The passengers came on board.

"Good morning, may I have your seat number?" the welcoming stewardess said in honeyed tones.

And then Kelly saw Steve climb on board.

"This is my future," she said to the girl at the gate. "Give this guy the red carpet treatment."

There was a double take and then a giggle. "Got it," the girl said. "Oh, my, he's terribly attractive, Kelly."

The 747, the Monster, cut across the sky above the Atlantic Ocean. In a short lull, Kelly sat with Steve. "Can I get you anything?" she asked.

"Not at the moment."

"Well, then," she said. "I have a little time to myself. And during that time, there are a few questions I'd like to have answers to."

"Yes, dear?"

"What's your racket?"

"What vulgar language from a Scarsdale girl."

"Shove it," she said. "I'm, for the last time, serious. What was your connection with Richard Comstock and relatives? Are you a dick?"

"A dick?" He frowned fastidiously.

"An eye, a private guy. Tell me."

"There's no mystery about it," he said. "My connection with the Comstock compound was purely personal. Richard's aunt Elizabeth is a friend of mine. She's almost fifty years old, but when her husband ditched her, she decided she wanted to get her Ph.D. So she's in one of my classes at Columbia. I teach English. Also Psychology. I have tenure. And a reasonably good salary. Just under seventeen thousand."

"You're putting me on," she said.

"Not at all. This is the truth. But of course there's something else. I write on the side. Crime stories. Very good little crime stories. You'll never starve, Kelly."

He smiled, and took her hand. "I want you to meet Aunt Elizabeth," he said. "You'll like her very much. She's the only member of the Comstock family who isn't a jerk. I mean, outside of Richard."

"Steve, I can't believe my ears. You mean you *teach?*"

"What's that, a dirty word?"

He kissed her, and then lit a cigar. "Yes, Richard's aunt was worried about him. So I promised to keep an eye on him in Spain. She's such an old darling, you'll like her."

She laughed. "Oh, Steve. And I thought you were C.I.A Or Mafia. You're a professor! You with your Humphrey Bogart act. A real tough guy. I could die laughing."

"They laughed at Fulton," he said. "And at Socrates, for that matter. But I notice those fellas had the last hee haw."

•••

It was six in the evening when they left Kennedy Airport in a taxi. The sky was pink and blue and promised a bright day for tomorrow. "These are the good days," Steve said. "Summer's coming in. I like this time of year."

"Me too."

They went through Queens, turning up toward Madison and the East Side.

"Your place or mine?" Steve asked.

"What?"

"You heard me."

She thought about it. And then she looked at him. It didn't really matter whose place. It would be their place before long. But when it happened, she decided, she would just as soon have it in her two rooms with the familiar objects surrounding her, so that she could guide Steve in every way possible into her life, knowing the shape of the boundaries in which she had existed for so long. And there lead him into their common future.

"Just off Madison," she told the driver. "Where those bright lights are to the left."

The cab pulled to a stop. She stood waiting, and the maple tree on the corner was in full leaf. It was an end, and a beginning. The taxi pulled away and Kelly reached out a hand.

"Watch the steps," she said, and helped him up. In the dusk they smiled at each other and went up the single flight that led into another time, another way of doing things, another life.

A Sneak Peek from Crimson Romance
(From *Viking Fire* by Andrea Cooper)

Ireland 856 CE

"I renounce Father for this." Kaireen threw the elderberry gown. Dressed only in her leine, she glared at the new gown on the stone floor.

"Shame on you and your children for speaking such." Her handmaid, Elva, gathered the damask and then dusted off the rushes. "It's a wonder one of the clim has not scolded you from your hearth for such talk." She wore her white hair twisted in a chignon, underneath a linen head cloth. Strands of white hair poked out the sides of her covering.

"No, curse Father for a fool." She plopped on her bed and a goose feather floated away. With a huff, she leaned against the oak headboard. Red curtains puffed like a robin's chest around oak poles supporting her wooden canopy.

Her bare feet brushed against the stone floor. Why was she not born plain like her two older sisters? Already they had married and expected their second bairns by spring. Well, at least so far she had enjoyed twenty years of freedom.

Three years longer than her sisters. Her parents had her sisters married by their seventeenth birthday. Marriage at such a late age was uncommon, but her father had wanted suitable matches. They had enjoyed freedom longer than others. Many women were given in marriage soon after their first woman's cycle.

Neither of her sisters had had matrimonial dreams of love matches. Both were arranged marriages. Margaret was married to an O'Neill. They courted through the long winter and past the blooming of spring with an early summer wedding.

Two months later he roamed other women's skirts, finding too many others who were willing. Margaret's irritation was lessened as she was ensured by the Laird O'Neill's formal letter that no bastard would have claim to her husband's land or rights if she were widowed.

Her other sister, Shay, and her husband did not set eyes upon each other until the wedding feast. Then they were never separated until tragedy ripped them apart.

Four months ago, her husband was killed in an unexpected skirmish against another clan. Shay refused to admit his death—until his blood-soaked body arrived with his clansmen.

For days she refused to eat or drink. Her salvation was she carried their second unborn child in her womb, and their two-year-old daughter needed a mother. The wee bairn was due this month. Kaireen feared that without the children, her sister would have wasted away without her love.

Often she wondered what her life would be like with a love like Shay's. A love so strong it threatened her sister's life . . . or would she prefer Margaret's marriage, without love and faithfulness?

"You know your da arranged a marriage within a season." Elva smirked.

Kaireen shook her head. "To another land holder," and waved a hand in disgust, "not t-this heathen. Twice they raided our land in the last month alone." She slapped away a strand of her auburn hair from her face. "Their forces choke the land like the town of Ath Cliath, the hurdled ford they call Dubhlinn." This was in reference to the bank of wooden hurdles the Vikings built across the Liffey River. Recent whispers of a possible spy in their midst sent shivers down Kaireen's back. What if this foreigner was the spy? What if he had fooled everyone in her clan?

Well, she would not have the wool pulled over her head by likes of a Lochlann.

"Many a raid has come from them. Now father wants me as wife to one of them?" She clenched her fists. "No, I will not marry this Viking or as we call his kind from west Scandia-Lochlanns." She snatched the green hazel twig from Elva's outstretched hand. Then she scrubbed her teeth.

When the foreigners had first attacked Ireland, they had been called Gaill. Over time the distinction grew between Gaills, Lochlanns, and Normanni depending on what part of Scandia they swooped down from.

Elva smiled, reminding Kaireen of the rumors of her handmaid's uncanny foresight. Whispers of Elva making strange things happen and often blamed as the cause of Kaireen's stubborn refusal to behave as a laird's daughter should.

Kaireen tossed the twig in the fire burning in the hearth. After taking the woolen cloth Elva handed her, she wiped her teeth.

"You've not seen him yet." Elva wiggled her brows.

"So?" Kaireen shrugged. "I would like to never see him." She scrubbed her teeth again with the woolen fabric, and then set the cloth aside.

"Well then, would you not like to know if you have a handsome husband or not?" She waited for her response, but Kaireen scowled at her. Elva chuckled. "I would rather get a good look at him now than the morning after."

Kaireen's ears heated. "I am not marrying." She shook her head for emphasis. "So there will be no morning, nor night, nor wedding."

"If he is handsome, I may fight you for him." Elva smiled, deepening the wrinkles around her eyes.

"Welcome to him either way." Kaireen laughed.

"Careful." Elva winked. "Love makes us fall hardest when we have no intention of doing so. "Especially if stubbornness or pride is involved." She fluffed the damask gown. "Up with you now. We cannot have you going for supper in your leine."

"With or without my leine, I do not go willingly." Kaireen rose. She allowed Elva to yank the violet gown over her head. She pushed her arms through and her clenched hands emerged out of the long sleeves.

She brushed her pale hands down the front of the pile-weaved material. She squared her shoulders and then slipped on her leather shoes.

Plopping on her wooden stool, she suffered though Elva fixing her hair.

As Elva brushed her auburn mane, she fidgeted. Despite refusing to marry this foreigner, her stomach did a flip at the thought. *After all the Lochlanns are good for nothing but raping and pillaging!* To be safe, she would bring her dagger with her. It was waiting for her on top of her cherry wood chest. She tucked the nervousness away as her being hungry. Her handmaid twisted her locks and weaved ribbons within the waist length strands.

Then she secured the end with a ribbon sewn with pearls. Elva gestured for her to rise. Kaireen did so reluctantly.

"Stand straight," Elva snapped.

Kaireen frowned but obeyed. At least Elva was better than her mother's handmaid, Rhiannon. Ever since Rhiannon came to the keep fifteen years ago, she had given Kaireen nightmares. Kaireen would have asked the fairies to put a changeling in her place if she had to have her care. Her mother tried to explain why they had accepted her into their clan being that she was an O'Neill, but Kaireen had tuned her out. She did not care where the woman was from or why.

"And stop scowling or I will throw you out the window with the chamber pot waste."

Her stomach tightened, but she bid Elva goodnight. She hiked up her gown to avoid tripping and then marched the corridor to the great hall.

Through her slippers, she felt the cold of the stone floor. A draft of wind coursed through her and she shuddered. She rounded the corner and forced her arms to her sides. She must appear strong and unnerved. Her arguments would hold no bearing if she could not stop shaking from fury.

• • •

Inside the banquet hall, the tables were covered with spiced apples, roasted carrots, asparagus, wild duck, quail, and foul smelling pig. Her father and mother sat next to each other at the middle of the high table.

Various lords, barons and their wives along with sons and daughters, laughed at an amusing story her father told. Three hunting dogs scampered around, devouring falling morsels. In a corner lay a fourth dog, shaggier than the rest gnawing on a bone.

Kaireen strolled to the low table, taking the empty seat on the bench across from her parents. Her favored place on her father's left was already taken by a stranger with golden hair, the Lochlann stared at her. Kaireen felt the urge to check the neckline of her gown, but stifled it. A servant girl refilled his goblet with ale.

Kaireen glanced back at him. Golden hair cascaded to his broad shoulders. His azure eyes unsettled her. Her breath caught in her throat and she jerked her head away from his gaze. Didn't the priest say something like "Breton, the devil that dragon often disguises himself as an angel of light." She had no desire to find out from which side of Sidhe, the fairy haven, this stranger sailed from.

Silently she admonished herself to stop playing the role of a child. Thought Elva might find him handsome, well, most women would. She heard women's gowns rustle as they leaned forward to catch a glimpse of the man from across the seas. The way these women gasped at his sailing story, any moment one of them would faint. Did they forget so soon that he was a Viking? One of many who ravaged their land, sacked their monasteries at best, and took women and children as slaves. Some of the women were fortunate enough not to be raped, others were not so lucky.

Her ears burned when the Lochann's resonant voice told of the fiery red dragon he tamed sailing their coast. Did her father tell him that he had always teased her that it would be easier for him to raise a red dragon then a red-haired daughter?

Her insides twisted as the Lochlann finished spinning his tale. She would not look at him again tonight. What did she care what his appearance was anyway. She took a sip of wine, glancing at the stranger over the rim.

He winked at her and she choked.

As the baroness on her left twisted, the bench creaked. She pounded Kaireen on the back with her palm. Her back bruised from the woman's smacks, she assured the woman she no longer needed assistance.

"What do you think of our country, Bram son of Ragnar?" her mother asked the Lochlann.

"Never seen anything so green. Until I looked into your daughter's eyes which make the trees bow in shame."

"Blasphemous." A blush flooded to the roots of Kaireen's hair.

"No, 'tis truth."

Her father held his cup in a toast. "To Bram, the first man ever to bring a blush to my daughter's cheeks."

Kaireen glowered, her anger filling her.

The hall rang with laughter. She wished for sap to stick their mouths shut.

After the laughter subsided, her father cleared his throat. "Now, now. We must control ourselves. Not every day a man gets his last child married."

"I am not marrying," Kaireen interrupted. "And I am not a child."

"Gracious Bram has agreed to stay on with us for a fortnight. Then he will marry our Kaireen."

The applause was deafening. She jumped off the bench, glaring at the Lochlann's smiling face.

"A fortnight?" she screeched. "Not enough time for me to… he is a foreigner and a Lochlann at that." Why did they believe it was suitable for her to marry this Viking? She had to have time to figure out how to get rid of him.

"How much time do you need?" her mother asked in a warning tone.

"Never would be too soon," Kaireen shot back.

"Enough." Her father slammed his fist on the table.

Before the ale spilled, her mother snatched her goblet. Their argument brought whispers through the tables.

Her father waved his drink and the ale sloshed on the linen tablecloth. "A fortnight was his idea. I wanted you wed tonight." Kaireen opened her mouth to protest, but his glare caused her to clamp it shut. "Further, you will wed Bram son of Ragnar and be happy about it. Or I will have you whipped until your ungrateful hide is stripped from you."

Kaireen fell on the bench with a groan. She did not need to look to know the Lochlann was beaming. Curse them all for fools. With her knife she pushed her piece of duck around on the trencher. She would not submit, no matter how much her father yelled.

After they finished the other five courses, her father ordered the musicians brought in. Servants scrambled to remove the tables and benches, making room for the dancers. The high table remained.

At Kaireen's orders, the servants placed her bench near the back of the high table so she faced away from the dancers.

The baroness continued to eat beside her; it was the subject of many jokes she would not finish her supper until the kitchens were empty.

Three lute players, and a harpist played the round dance song.

Soon, Kaireen tapped her foot to the rhythm. She watched her father and mother, along with many of the other guests, whirl through the hall changing partners within the lines. The foreigner danced among them.

The oldest woman grinned, as though he were her suitor when he took her arm. Rebecca, a year younger than Kaireen, circled around twice in a row with him.

"It matters not to me who he dances with. Maybe he will change his mind and marry her," she muttered.

She smirked, envisioning his astonishment at learning that Rebecca's dark mane was a wig. Rebecca's hair, a stringy brown, had been chopped off three years ago. No one knew exactly why, but ever since her bout of sickness, patches of baldness showed through her hair, which refused to grow again.

But Kaireen's eyes followed him across the floor. He released Rebecca into the women's line. After he turned, he waved for Kaireen to join him. She whipped her head back to face the table.

Her skin prickled. She bit her lip, suppressing the notion that she had been caught staring. She snatched a piece of duck and ate.

The baroness stood and Kaireen held onto the bench to keep from falling to the floor. The music changed twice while Kaireen was brooding, but she determined she would not turn around again. She would wait until the next song, and then retire. Therefore, he would know she was neither afraid nor interested in him.

Across the room, she heard Rebecca's laughter. She wanted to scream and rip the girl's wig off, exposing her. However, she remained in her seat, her back rigid.

She congratulated herself on her discipline, when Elva appeared from nowhere at her side.

"Must not let the night pass without a dance." She pulled on Kaireen's elbow.

"I have no wish to," Kaireen protested.

Her voice fell on deaf ears, for Elva yanked her to stand.

Her handmaid pushed her forward. Kaireen's slippers slid across the stone floor as she tried to dig in her heels.

"Stop, or I will have you locked in the stocks." She turned her head to yell at her handmaid.

A male hand grasped her arm and escorted her through the line. Her attention shifted as she glared at a beaming Elva. She saw her handmaid skip from the hall.

Then Kaireen glanced at her partner.

Bram held her.

She tripped, but he steadied her. His hands were warm.

"Careful." His dark sapphire eyes twinkled. She wondered if one could drown gazing up into their depths. "People will think you swoon for me."

Her face heated with anger, she believed her skin colored purple. She stamped her foot on his boot, but he did not flinch. She tried to jerk away from his grip, but he held her firmly.

"Let me go." She looked around for help, but everyone had given them a wide berth. They danced around the pair, smiling and nodding as if she and Bram were a happy couple. "'Tis my turn in the line again."

"No." He led her to the balcony.

Outside he released her, but blocked her path to re-enter the hall.

The music resonated around them. Leaning against the far wall, she crossed her arms. She was two feet away from him, but he was too close.

"I thought the air would clear your head." He cocked his eyebrow, examining her.

"My head is fine, thank you."

"Aye, and the rest of you is fine to look at too." His thick dialect chased shivers through her.

Her hands smoothed her gown. She caught herself and stopped. At seeing his grin, her frown deepened. "I believe it's improper for you to stare at a lady so."

"Would you rather I stare at you on our wedding night?" She opened her mouth to speak, but he continued. "Whilst you are without clothes?"

"I assure you, sir, we will have no wedding night." Her blush radiated from her chest and spread between her legs.

"You wish to wed during the day then?" He took a step closer. "Very well, daylight will be all the better to see you."

Music and laughter from inside filtered through the night air. He strode toward her.

She braced for his advances, wondering if she had the strength to inflict enough pain to make him reconsider. Part of her wanting to run, the other part daring him closer in challenge. God's toenails, how could she have forgotten her dagger?

A breath from her, he stopped. Her heart hammered in her chest.

His fingers brushed aside a strand of her auburn hair that had slipped from her braid.

The brief touch sent fire coursing through her. Afraid her legs would give way she leaned back against the wall. He did have a wonderful smile though, with full lips and small white scar that went from his lower lip to his chin.

If he kissed her, she would like nothing more than to bite through those lips leaving another scar far worse than the one he already bore. Or her dagger would have been enough to keep his lips at bay. Why had she forgotten it when Elva dressed her?

Best to make him leave, and soon. He watched her for what felt like an eternity.

"Sir, you take far too many liberties." Her eyes darted behind him at the dancing. Rebecca craned her neck to see what they did outside the great hall unescorted. "Others…" Kaireen began, but she stopped seeing anger flare in his eyes.

"I take none." His mouth firmed. "You are to be my wife. I take liberties with no one else."

His voice stung her. He spun on his heel and left her gaping after him.